CROSSING

JORDAN

BY

Dan Good

Crossing Jordan
© 2017 Dan Good

Table of Contents

Chapter 1

As he approached the City limits, Ben immediately saw the sign that read "Welcome to Jordan, Population 7,800". Seeing the sign, he felt compelled to pull over and stop. There was a wide shoulder just ahead of the sign, so he pulled his jeep and U-Haul trailer off the road. "Jordan", that reminded him of the Old Testament story of when the Israelites had crossed the Jordan River. Having wandered in the desert for years, the Israelites were preparing for a new beginning, a new way of life. They knew that once they crossed the river, there would be no turning back. Ben had not been traveling as long as the Israelites, but his two day, 1200 mile drive from Cleveland, Ohio to Jordan, Kansas had seemed like an endless journey. This little town in the northwest corner of Kansas would be a new beginning for him, just what he wanted. He was ready to distance himself from the emotions and stress that had come upon his life during the past year. Now he knew there was no turning back. He couldn't continue to relive the …..

Ben suddenly came out of his trance and noticed the time on his watch. It was 3:00 p.m. He needed to be moving on in order to make his 3:30 p.m. appointment with Mr. Reed, the high school Principal. Ben always prided himself in never being late. He certainly didn't want to be late for this meeting. Mr. Reed had given him instructions to the school, which should be easy to follow, especially in a small town like Jordan. But none the less, he didn't want to make a bad impression by being late.

Chapter 2

Ben found the school easily and was actually fifteen minutes early. He debated about going in right away, but thought it better not to be too early. During his short wait in the parking lot he observed that the school had been around for a long time. The building was constructed of dark colored brick – all one color. It was a multi-story building with large windows on each floor. The windows were trimmed with white boards, at least in the building's earlier days. Now the trim was in severe need of a paint job. There were wide concrete steps at the entrance to the building that were cracked in several locations. The handrails were bent and also in dire need of paint. The landscaping probably once looked very appealing, but now the flowering plants were dwarfed by grass and weeds. The bushes had obviously not been trimmed in several years and several appeared half dead. The parking lot, originally asphalt, was in serious disrepair. Much of the area had been reduced to gravel and there were very few apparent parking lines.

Nearing his appointment time, Ben entered the school through the two large doors at the top of the steps. Once inside he immediately noticed the aged hardwood floors with spots and scratches that polish had obviously not removed. Outdated metal lockers lined each side of the hallway and an ancient looking water fountain with a rubber mat under it to catch the over shooting water was located at the end of the row of lockers. He saw a sign for the Principal's Office about half way down the hallway. The door was made with very dark stained wood. At the top of the door was a frosted glass window. As Ben opened the door he was immediately greeted by an elderly woman with wire rimmed glasses slid half way down her nose. Her facial expression was very un-welcoming as she gruffly asked, "What do you want?"

Ben noticed the name plate on her desk which read "Mrs. Grimm". How appropriate, he thought! Ben tried to suppress his negative emotions as he replied as politely as he could, "I am Ben Harper and I have a 3:30 appointment with Mr. Reed."

"It isn't on my calendar! Does Mr. Reed know that? ", she responded harshly. Before Ben could muster a reply, she got up and entered Mr. Reed's office, closing the door behind her. After nearly a ten minute wait, which seemed like more of an intentional delay than a need to conclude any activity on the part of Mr. Reed, the elderly woman emerged and ushered Ben into Mr. Reed's office.

Mr. Reed's office was horribly in disarray. There were stacks of papers all over his desk, to the extent that he could not read or write anything unless he pulled the slide board out from under his center drawer. There were books and reports all over the floor. Mr. Reed had to remove several documents from his visitor's chair before Ben could even sit down. Obviously, Mr. Reed didn't have many visitors!

Mr. Reed didn't formally introduce himself, but immediately began by mechanically reviewing all of the necessary paperwork and requirements for new teachers. Most of the paperwork was typical of what Ben had experienced at his previous job as a science teacher at Cleveland Central High School. Mr. Reed continued, "And now I must make you aware of a couple other issues. One, you must make sure that every student passes your class. We are not a babysitting service here at Jordan High. Your goal is to get them in and get them out, no matter what it takes. Do you get what I mean?" Ben wasn't sure he understood what he had just heard, but it sounded like he was expected to falsify grades, if necessary, to make sure no one failed. Ben was a man of integrity and cheating was not something he could support.

Before he could even ask for clarification, Mr. Reed said, "And two, there is absolutely no tolerance in our school for teachers praying or talking about God. Any violation of this policy on school property will be grounds for immediate termination. Consider this your only warning. Your text books are in your room. They are a bit outdated, but that is all we have. You are free to teach what you want, just make sure I only see passing grades. Mrs. Grimm will show you to your classroom. Have a good day, Mr. Harper.

Welcome to Jordan High." Not exactly the welcome Ben had expected, but apparently it would have to do.

Ben's classroom was on the second floor, which was even less inviting than the first floor. His classroom certainly lacked the conveniences of any modern technology. There were no interactive white boards, no video projection equipment, no computers, just rows of wooden chairs - the type with the wrap around desk top and book storage underneath. Most of them were well worn and certainly did not appear very comfortable. Up front was a large old oak desk, which was cleared of all papers and books. It was stained a dark color, but it was obvious that it had been through many years of service. It was accompanied by an old wooden desk chair of matching color and age. There was a thin pillow on the seat, which Ben assumed meant that it was not very comfortable either.

Ben was now alone. Mrs. Grimm had returned to her den, presumably to welcome any other unsuspecting visitors. He was glad to be alone. He needed some time to process all that had just transpired. In less than 15 minutes he had walked into a school building that probably wouldn't comply with even half of the current building code requirements, he had encountered two of the most unfriendly people he had ever met, and now he was totally alone in an antiquated room that was to be his place of work for months to come.

Ben began to wonder if he had gotten himself into a bad situation. Perhaps he had acted too hastily in making such a drastic change, but a change is what he wanted – so he thought.

Chapter 3

Last Christmas had been extremely difficult for Ben, and that coupled with stressful relationships had caused him to look for another teaching position, at a school far away from where he was. He needed a new beginning. So he began an internet search for schools out west. There were several possibilities in larger towns, but he felt that a smaller school would be more appealing. Finally in late April he found an opening for a high school science teacher in Jordan, Kansas. Science was his subject of expertise, so he was very interested. He reviewed the web site for the high school, but wasn't able to learn very much. It was not a very professional web page and the information was very limited. None-the-less he submitted his resume with his letter of interest, and then waited. After nearly two weeks, Ben received an e-mail requesting a telephone interview. Ben had nearly given up, since there had been no response. But now, the anticipation of an interview caused him to get excited. The semester at Cleveland High ended at the end of May, so he had a lot of work to do in preparing final exams, grading reports, and helping some of the slower students with their homework. He had very little time to prepare for an interview.

The interview was scheduled for 4:00 p.m. on Friday after school. He planned his schedule to be at his apartment in plenty of time in case the school called early. At 4:05 the phone finally rang. It was Mr. Reed, the school Principal for Jordan High, and two school board members; Mr. Phelps, the School Board President, and Mr. Higgins, a School Board member. The interview was brief and to the point. They were in desperate need of a teacher, and Ben was in desperate need of a new job. Without inquiring much about the details, he accepted their offer and agreed to meet with Mr. Reed at 3:30 p.m. on June 5, only a week after the semester ended at Cleveland High.

Jordan was on a year round trimester plan, which meant the summer session began on June 8. He knew he couldn't take much with him, since he planned to pull a U-Haul trailer. Fortunately, he was able to sell most of his appliances and larger furniture items in the short time that he had. He then packed up the rest of his belongings and headed for Jordan.

The school at Cleveland was in a fairly well-to-do suburb with a healthy tax base. As a result, he had enjoyed the amenities of a fairly new school, which had been equipped with the latest technology. He began his career there and had taken all of these conveniences as the norm. At Jordan he felt like he had traveled back in time 20 to 30 years. This school had no current day features. He could see that his teaching style would have to change drastically.

Chapter 4

After a cursory review of the textbooks and science equipment, Ben left the school around 4:45 p.m. His next stop was to check in with his new landlord, Mrs. Campbell. Once Ben had accepted the teaching offer, he did an internet search in an attempt to find an apartment or small house that he could rent. There were only a few listings with some limited photos. Most looked a bit run down, but he did find one small house that had a pleasant appearance and was located just outside of town. Since he only had a few days to find something, he quickly made a phone call to the number listed on the website. He was instantly greeted with a friendly voice. He explained that he was a single school teacher moving very soon to Jordan to teach at the high school. Mrs. Campbell indicated that the house was still available, but she was hesitant to rent to single men, knowing the party atmosphere they often brought with them. Ben understood her concern but did his best to assure her that he wasn't a party person, and that he would take good care of her property. After extensive questioning, Mrs. Campbell finally agreed to rent her house to Ben.

Mrs. Campbell lived in a small home about a quarter mile down the road from her rental property. Ben spotted her house up ahead. Her directions had been flawless and he arrived right at 5:00 p.m. Mrs. Campbell must have been waiting, because she walked out on the porch as soon as Ben pulled in front of her house. Ben jumped out of his jeep and walked toward the porch. Her home was quaint and picturesque. It was obviously well maintained and numerous flowers ordained the front and sides of her house. A couple ornamental trees had been strategically planted adjacent to the sidewalk. It was a friendly house and Ben could tell by the bright smile on Mrs. Campbell's face that she was also a friendly person. Her smile was genuine, warm and inviting, and he would come to learn that it was characteristic of her life. He could tell even before hearing her speak that she was going to be a good friend. She was medium build with well groomed white hair, a mark of wisdom he thought. She was slightly on the short side but obviously in good physical shape. He would guess her age to be around 75.

"Mr. Harper," she said as she walked closer. "I'm glad to see that you made it to Jordan. How was your trip?"

"It was a long drive, but I made it OK. Your directions were perfect. I was able to drive straight to your house."

After exchanging some get-acquainted dialogue, she took him down the road to her rental house. The house was as equally inviting as Mrs. Campbell's house. It was also well maintained and very clean. It had two nice sized bedrooms and a moderately sized kitchen with fairly up-to-date appliances. The dining room and living room were one large open area. The furniture was the only defining difference between the two spaces. The house had a two car garage and a good sized yard, which was growing vigorously.

"Mrs. Campbell," Ben began. But before he could continue, Mrs. Campbell interrupted him.

"Please call me Ruth, no need for formalities around here."

Ben acknowledged her request and responded, "Well Ruth, please call me Ben."

Ruth offered to help Ben carry some of his things from the U-Haul into the house. As they were talking Ben asked, more out of the need for conversation than from genuine interest, "How is it that a single lady, like yourself, has rental property like this?" Noticing her hesitation, he suggested that they sit down on the back of the U-Haul to rest for a few minutes.

Ruth began, "My husband and I used to live in this house, until five years ago. For several months he hadn't been feeling well. He went to several doctors, but they were unable to determine what was wrong. When he took a turn for the worse, the doctors did more extensive testing and found that he was in the latter stages of cancer. He passed away a few weeks later. This house was bigger than I needed, so I put it on the market, but the housing market in Jordan hasn't been very good for a long time. I had some interest, but no good offers. The house where I live now came up for sale at a reasonable price, so I decided to buy it and rent this one until I could find a serious buyer. The memories associated with this house were too difficult for me to cope with at the time. I thought a different house would help. At any rate, I'm happy where I am. It was a difficult time in my life, but God gave me the strength I needed to make it through."

Ben could see the tears in her eyes and regretted that he had asked the question. "I'm sorry, Ruth, I didn't mean to bring up painful memories."

They continued unpacking his things in silence for a while. As the mood lightened a bit, Ruth asked, "Did you have a chance to meet with Mr. Reed yet?"

"Yes, in fact I just came from the school. I had a 3:30 appointment with him. Our meeting was a bit awkward, to say the least. He seemed very preoccupied, and he was certainly less than friendly." Ben suddenly wondered if he had said more than he should have. What if Ruth and Mr. Reed were good friends? He probed a little and asked, "Do you know him?"

Ruth paused for a moment and then began. "Mr. Reed has been at Jordan High for a long time. In his early years he was really focused on building relationships with the students and with the teachers. But lately he has changed. A lot of the students at Jordan High don't excel academically. It is just the nature of this community. About three years ago the State Board of Education came to town and performed an audit of the entire high school; material being taught, student-teacher ratio, performance on standardized tests, and a lot of other things. Anyway, they gave the school and Mr. Reed in particular a very bad report. Too many kids were skipping classes and test scores were very low. The School Board almost terminated him, but ultimately decided to give him one more chance to turn things around. Mr. Reed plans to retire in a few years and if he is fired he will lose his teacher's pension. That is one of our State laws."

Ben replied, "That helps explain some of his comments when I met with him earlier this afternoon. He warned me that I must make sure every student passed, regardless of what it took. I think he was telling me to falsify scores, if necessary, so that no one would fail. I've always tried to do what is right. I certainly hope this doesn't become an issue."

After a moment of silence Ruth said, "Don't worry, Ben, God never lets the righteous fall[1]."

Ben pondered that thought as he continued unpacking and moving his things into the house. They continued unloading items together until Ruth had to leave for a church meeting. Ben thanked Ruth for her help. He sensed that Ruth was a lady of great wisdom.

---

[1] Ps. 55:22 – Cast your cares on the Lord and He will sustain you; He will never let the righteous be shaken. (NIV)

Chapter 5

Ben spent the next couple days getting his house arranged, stocking up on needed groceries, and preparing lessons for the start of school. The textbooks were considerably different than what he had been used to using, so preparations were taking longer than he expected. He also spent some time in his classroom getting familiar with what science equipment was available, and what was not available. To Ben's dismay he found that the school really didn't have much equipment, and the equipment the school did have was very outdated and badly worn. He would have to make do knowing that at this late date it would be impossible for the school to approve the purchase of anything new.

It was now Wednesday night and Ben was exhausted from the long drive, moving into his house, unpacking, and trying to get ready for the first day of school. The hectic schedule left little time for thoughts about anything else, especially last year. That was a good thing!

Ben got up early Thursday morning, ate a quick breakfast, and put on a dress shirt, nice slacks, and a tie – his typical school attire. He said a quick prayer for God's help on this first day, and then he hurried to school in order to be there well before any of the students. He busied himself straightening the rows of desks until it was time for class to begin. He was a little nervous, not knowing quite what to expect in a new school. As the first students entered the room, it was obvious they were giving him the once over look. Ben did a quick appraisal of the students, also, seeing what he hadn't anticipated. There was obviously no dress code at Jordan High. Kids were wearing shorts and t-shirts with all kinds of weird and obnoxious pictures on them, torn jeans, and flip flops or grossly dirty tennis shoes. Many of the boys had hair longer than the girls. Caps seemed popular and hair colors matched the rainbow.

This was not at all like Cleveland where the students were expected to dress nicely and be respectable. It appeared that any rules of this sort had not been enforced for a long time, if ever.

After some hesitation, Ben called the class to order and introduced himself. "Good morning. I'm Mr. Harper, your new science teacher. I recently moved from Cleveland, Ohio, and I'm looking forward to this semester as we study science together. It will take me a few days to learn your names, but in order to help me get acquainted I would like each of you to state your name and then tell me one thing that you really enjoy doing. Let's start over here on my left. Would you start, please?"

The first girl began, "My name is Jamie Blye and I like boys!"

"Jamie, that is nice, but the question was 'What do you like to do, not what do you like'."

"Oh," Jamie said. "I'm sorry. I like playing with boys!" That brought a lot of chatter from others in the class, especially the boys. Things were not getting off to a good start, but Ben continued through the rest of the students. Many were intentionally trying to embarrass him. Others were more serious and were trying to legitimately answer Ben's "get acquainted" question. Some of the legitimate answers included horseback riding, working on trucks, painting, playing football, and cooking. Ben wrote down each student's name and response, thinking it might prove beneficial in future conversations.

It appeared that less than half the class was even remotely interested in school, let alone science. But it was too early to make that assessment. He was optimistic.

The first two days of school, Thursday and Friday, were more of an endurance test for Ben than a science class. Every time he would try to lecture, the kids would start heckling him about his necktie, his shoes, or anything else that came to mind. Several students would pass notes even when Ben was looking. Boys sitting behind girls would pull their hair or poke them in the back. Some read comic books while others were drawing pictures in their notebooks. Ben was not a strong disciplinarian. He knew that was not a characteristic of his DNA. His approach had always been to show love and compassion rather than cold force. But seeing the attitude of these kids, he was now questioning if his "meek and mild" approach was going to work. He didn't want to send kids to the Principal, since that sent the message that he was unable to control his own students. That would probably make matters worse, plus the kids would not be in class, losing any hope of learning what they really needed to know.

Ben had a few opportunities to meet some of the teachers between classes and during lunch time. Most were 50 years old or older, not overly friendly, and did not display any outward joy in their jobs. Negative attitudes seemed to be the norm. This mentality of the students and teachers was quite contrary to Ben's previous teaching experience. He had always felt the goal of teaching was to be a positive example to the students, to encourage them to learn, and to stimulate them to prepare for their futures. In only a couple days, Ben was quickly learning that these things were not the focus of the Jordan High students or staff.

Ben lectured his way through the first chapter of the book, enduring the sarcastic remarks and lack of interest by many of the students. On Thursday he gave a quiz over what they had studied so far. The quiz was announced ahead of time so that everyone would have ample time to study. The quiz was fairly short and very easy for anyone who read the book and listened in class. As Ben handed out the quiz, there were moans of "Why do we have to do this? You are being too hard on us. Give us a break. None of the other teachers give quizzes in the first two weeks of school, how come you are?"

Ben ignored the comments and continued. Ben collected the papers at the end of the period and then dismissed the class. As Ben graded the papers during his break period, he felt sadness and disappointment flood his emotions. Over 70% of the class failed the quiz. They obviously were not even trying. The next day Ben returned the graded quizzes to the students. They were appalled that Ben had given them failing grades. Negative comments were prolific, but one statement hit Ben hard.

"You can't fail us. That is against school policy. You will lose your job if you flunk us."

That thought had been in the back of his mind ever since he met with the school Principal when he arrived in Jordan, but he didn't realize that the students knew the Principal's requirement. Ben paused in silence for several seconds, collecting his thoughts before he responded. "My job as a teacher is to prepare you for the future, to be responsible adults that will make a positive difference in the world. I am more concerned about you being successful with your lives than I am about losing my job. The grade I give you will be the grade you earn. If you disagree with this approach, you are free to leave this class, but beware that by doing so I will report a failing grade to the Principal at the end of the semester." Ben knew he was probably pushing the limit, but no one left, and for that he was glad.

16

Chapter 6

The weekend finally arrived – none too quick for Ben. He was exhausted from the stress of the classroom, the effort of preparing all new lessons, and just the negative attitude of the entire school. It was like a black hole that was sucking Ben into its infinite depths.

Mid morning on Saturday Ben's doorbell rang. When Ben opened the door, he was pleasantly surprised to see Ruth standing there with a plate of chocolate chip cookies, still warm from the oven. It lifted Ben's spirit to see a friendly smile.

"I thought you might like a sweet snack," Ruth said. "I hope you like chocolate chip."

Ben replied with saliva starting to build in his mouth, "Chocolate chip happens to be my favorite. Please come in Ruth. Thank you so much. I needed something refreshing after the last few days."

Ben invited Ruth to sit down at the kitchen table, and they enjoyed the cookies together. Ben had some milk in the refrigerator, so he complimented her cookies with his milk.

Ruth began, "How did school go this week, Ben?"

Ben needed to talk about it, more than he realized, and Ruth was a good listener. "It was far from what I expected," Ben said. "The kids were very unruly, there is no respect for teachers or for fellow students, they don't seem to care about learning, and even the other faculty members have horrible attitudes. These kids are hopeless." Ben suddenly realized that last sentence didn't come out quite right. "I mean, it seems these kids don't have any hope. They are just biding their time with no direction on where they want to go."

After a bit of a pause, reflecting on what Ben had just said, Ruth replied. "Jordan used to be a thriving town. Everyone had a decent job, our economy was good, the schools were good, there were after school activities for the kids, and there was very little crime in our town. That all changed a few years ago when American Fabrication went out of business. AF employed hundreds of people. They made parts for various companies throughout the world. Most of the town was either employed by AF or by a business that supported AF. People weren't wealthy, but AF provided a decent living for most people, and they had good benefits. Attitudes were good and people enjoyed living here. When the economy went downhill, the demand for parts tapered off drastically. Ultimately the company had to close its doors. They only gave their employees two week's notice – their jobs ended almost over night! There were no termination benefits and no help in finding other jobs. It was like life in Jordan stopped. AF's tax dollars were the major source of funding for the schools. So when the funding stopped, the schools suffered dramatically. The heartbeat of the community was gone. Everyone was full of stress and negative attitudes. Thirty to forty percent of our population left seeking jobs elsewhere. Those that stayed have suffered many hardships. You are right, Ben, not only are the students hopeless, so are the parents. They feel trapped with no way out. For many, they have given up even trying."

"Wow, what a sad situation. When I accepted the offer to teach here, I had no idea things were like this."

"Had you known ahead of time, would that have changed your mind?" Ruth inquired. She could sense that Ben was different than the other teachers she knew and the short term ones that had rented her house in the past. Once they found out Jordan's situation, they were quick to move to other places.

Ben said, "Probably not. I was desperate for a change and Jordan seemed like a good opportunity." He hesitated for a moment and then continued. "When I was in Cleveland everything was going great. Amy, my wife, and I met in college and soon became deeply in love. We were both planning to be teachers, so we had a lot of classes together. Amy was a Christian girl with deep convictions. I was more of the 'life is what it is' type of guy. Over time Amy's faith rubbed off on me and I accepted Christ as my

18

Savior during my junior year. We became engaged and set our wedding date for June, after we graduated. We got married as planned. We both were able to get teaching jobs in Cleveland. She was a grade school teacher and I taught in the high school. We both loved kids and were excited to see them grow and learn new things. We felt we were doing what God wanted us to do. Last September Amy was driving through an intersection on her way to school when an elderly man had a heart attack and was unable to stop for a red light. He hit her car broadside on the driver's side door. Amy was killed instantly. My life was forever changed that day. I took a couple weeks off from school. Somehow I made it through the funeral, but I was really struggling. I knew God was in control, but I couldn't see the purpose in taking my beloved wife. We had a great marriage and she was having a wonderful impact on all of her students. They loved her dearly.

"After that, school was really hard for me. Not only was it difficult to focus, but nobody knew what to say to me. For the first couple days the other teachers and students expressed their sympathy, but after that it seemed that most people tried to avoid me. I know it was uncomfortable for them, and it became very awkward for me. It was like I was on my own little island. Things improved a little with time, but it never got back to the way it had been. Every night when I went home, our house seemed so empty. Amy was not there. I could no longer talk to her or share my day with her. That is when I decided I needed a new beginning – a new place to live, a new school, and new people to be around. I rationalized that far away where people didn't know me would be the ideal place. So, I began to search the internet and that is how I found Jordan. But after the last few days of school, I'm wondering if I made a wise decision. Teaching is my passion, but I don't know how to teach these kids."

"Ben, I'm so sorry to hear about your wife. That is a lot for you to endure at such a young age. I understand the feelings of isolation and not being able to have friends that can relate to you. But, time does heal things. You thought you made plans to move here and teach, but it was God who actually directed your steps and paved the way[2]. God has a purpose for every problem, even though we may not understand it."

"Thank you, Ruth, for listening to my story. It helps to just talk about it, especially with someone like you who has been through it yourself. I really want to make a difference in the lives of these kids, but it seems impossible."

"Ben, always remember that nothing is impossible with God[3]! God will show you a way."

Ben was encouraged by her optimism, but he still had his doubts. They continued their conversation for a while longer, enjoying the fresh cookies, but even more the freedom to share their thoughts and feelings with each other.

Ben knew he somehow had to change his approach with his students, but how? That was the big question. He prayed for God to show him the way.

---

[2] Prov. 16:9 – A man's heart plans his way, but the Lord directs his steps. (NKJV)
[3] Jer. 32:27 – "I am the Lord, the God of all mankind. Is anything too hard for me?" (NIV)

Chapter 7

Ben spent the majority of the weekend trying to figure out what he could change to make class time more exciting and fun. He needed things that would draw the students to class, not force them to class. Several ideas were starting to gel in his mind.

Monday morning came and Ben was filled with new enthusiasm. He arrived in his classroom well before school started. His first change was to arrange all of the desks in a circle around the room, including his own. His goal was to have all the students facing each other so that they might have better interaction and fewer opportunities to hassle each other. This would also give Ben a much better vantage point.

When the students arrived, they were shocked to see the new arrangement, but Ben encouraged them to find a seat. He could hear them mumbling a few negative comments, but eventually everyone found a seat and sat down. Ben began, "I want us to start over, a new beginning so to speak. I detect a lot of negative attitudes and a lot of apathy toward school. We need to change those thoughts – they are not healthy for you as young people, nor are they healthy for you as you get older. We need to be an encouragement to one another, not a discouragement. I've arranged the desks so we can all see each other. I think that will stimulate better communication.

"I've also given a lot a thought to this and I want to try taking about 10 minutes at the start of every class period to discuss whatever you would like to talk about. This should be an open discussion by everyone, and it should not be argumentative. It is intended to help us think and work together. So, for today, since you have not had time to prepare for this, I want each of you to take a piece of paper and write on it one positive thing about Jordan High School. Do not put your name on the paper. When you have written down one thing, fold the paper in half and pass them around to me. Then hopefully, we will have some food for thought."

"Mr. Harper, what if I can't think of anything positive?" asked one student.

Ben merely replied, "Think hard. I'm confident that you can come up with one thing."

Ben collected the papers and began to silently read through them. "We have electricity." "The school hasn't fallen down yet." "We have indoor plumbing." The first three were not what Ben was hoping to receive, but he continued to read. "We have smart teachers." "School is a nice place to come to get away from home." To avoid reading some of the more sarcastic comments to the class, Ben said. "In the essence of time I'm just going to read a few of these." As he read them, there were a few snide comments, but in general most everyone shook their head in agreement.

After reading several, Ben said, "Let's talk about this one, 'School is a nice place to get away from home.' Why would you want to get away from home?" Ben wasn't sure what responses he would get, but he needed to start some classroom interaction.

One student said, "There is nothing to do at home. My parents don't have much money, so all we do is sit around and watch TV." Another said, "My parents are always arguing. Home is not fun." Ben noticed several heads shaking on that one. Another said, "My dad lost his job and no one is happy anymore."

Ben was touched as he listened to their depressing comments. It sounded like many of these kids didn't have anything to look forward to in their lives. Somehow, he wished he could change things. "Thank you for sharing those comments. I don't have answers for these situations, but I know it does help to talk about them. Tomorrow we'll continue with another topic for our discussion time."

"So," Ben said, "we need to begin our science class. Before we start this chapter, let's step back and define what science is. According to the dictionary, science is the knowledge of the physical or material world gained through observation and experimentation.

In other words it is learning about how the world works. That means science is critical to almost all aspects of life. As part of our learning, I've decided that we are going to focus more on experimentation. We are actually going to do experiments to help us understand how the laws of the universe function – and how those laws affect us every day." The kids seemed to perk up a little when they heard Ben's new approach.

The next day the kids entered the class with more enthusiasm, Ben thought. Once seated, he again asked them to take out a piece of paper. "For today I want you to look at the person on your right, and write one positive thing about him or her. Do not write your name on the paper and do not use the person's name. Just refer to the person as he or she or him or her. Then fold the paper in half and pass them to me."

Some responses were not appropriate to read. Ben passed over those quickly. Many were very kind and complimentary. Those Ben read and praised the students for their encouraging comments. One of Ben's goals was that the students would start to bond together. It appeared that things were slowly beginning to improve.

Buck, the biggest student in the class, tall, husky, and obviously a bully type, began to torment Johnny, a shy and much smaller student. After a couple of warnings, the tormenting continued and so did his attitude of disrespect for Ben.

Ben finally said, "Buck that is enough. You cannot harass other students and disrupt this class. I can either send you down to the Principal's office for discipline or you can be disciplined here in class. Class, what is your preference?" Ben knew that if they chose the Principal, Buck would merely leave school for the rest of the day.

They all responded, "Do it here!"

"OK, then. Buck, go stand in the corner of the room facing the wall. Do not sit down, do not turn your head, and do not goof off in any way. If you do, the consequences will get much worse." Ben had no plan if Buck did any of those things, but he hoped the threat would be enough to keep him in compliance. The students began to laugh and snicker as Buck slowly migrated to the corner. This was a first for Buck. No one had ever really challenged him before. None of the students knew what to expect next.

Ben went to his desk and took out a sheet of plain paper. He began to write on the paper as the students watched quietly. He then walked over to the corner where Buck was standing and taped the paper to Buck's back. He told Buck not to turn around or remove the paper. The writing on the paper was small enough that no one could read it from their desk. Ben said, "I want each of you to walk single file behind Buck and then return to your seat."

The kids were still poking fun at Buck as he stood motionless in the corner. But as each one filed past Buck and read the note, the room grew tremendously silent. The note read, "Buck has done a wrong thing and deserves to be punished. If you have never in your entire life done anything wrong, then you may laugh at Buck[4]. Otherwise, count your blessings that you are not being punished." No one made a sound as they walked past. When everyone was back in their seats, Ben removed the paper from Buck's back and told Buck to take his seat. Buck had no idea what had just happened, but he detected a whole new attitude in the class. Not until after class did one of his buddies reveal the message on the paper. After that day, Ben had no problems with unruly students in his room. Each student gained a new insight and held Ben in much higher respect.

---

[4] John 8:7b – "Let any one of you who is without sin be the first to throw a stone at her." (NIV)

Chapter 8

Things were going much better in class. The students had been showing a much greater interest in the science lessons, and they especially seemed to enjoy the 10 minute open discussions prior to the lesson time.

The next chapter in the science book was on the origins of the universe with primary emphasis on the Big Bang Theory. Ben felt a churning is his stomach as he thought about the predicament he was now facing. Fortunately, Ben had another weekend to think about what to do. He remembered clearly the stern warning by the Principal that he could not teach or even talk about God, but somehow he had to convince the students that the Big Bang Theory was not true, that God in His sovereignty had created all things. He prayed, "Lord help me to have wisdom in obeying the school rules, but also in teaching the truth. Help me to be faithful to you, to honor you in all things."

Ben needed to stop by Ruth's house and pay her for the rent. It wasn't due for a few days, but he didn't like to cut it too close. Ruth answered the door with her normal cheerful smile. Just to be around her was always an encouragement. As Ben was giving her the rent check, she inquired, "How is school going, Ben?"

"I think things have improved a lot the last couple weeks. The kids have been more responsive and seem more enthused about learning. Their grades are improving, which is a good thing! Please pray for me this week, though. The next chapter we have to study is on the Big Bang Theory. As a Christian, I can't bring myself to teach the kids this. "

"I remember you telling me that Mr. Reed doesn't allow any teaching about God. That makes teaching the truth rather difficult. Maybe," she said, "if you can't teach them what is true you can teach them what isn't true."

With that comment, Ben suddenly had an idea. "Thanks, Ruth, you're a gem! I've got some work to do this weekend. I'd better get going. Thanks again. Talk to you later."

Ruth wasn't sure why Ben was suddenly so anxious to leave, but she knew he was on to something. She continued to pray for him.

Ben's mission, since he couldn't talk about how God created the universe according to the account in Genesis, was to prove that the Big Bang Theory couldn't be true. Perhaps this would help open the eyes of his students and make them think objectively and not just take for granted someone's idea. To accomplish his plan he needed to create a small explosion, but he didn't want any chance of someone getting injured. After thoughtful consideration, Ben headed for the fire station located in the center of town. Since it was run by volunteers, he hoped someone would be there. He pulled up and noticed a couple of trucks parked in the lot. He entered the station and found two men sitting in an office drinking coffee.

Frank and Jim greeted Ben warmly and introduced themselves. In response Ben introduced himself. "Hi, I'm Ben Harper, the new science teacher at the high school."

"We are glad to meet you, Ben. Are you interested in signing up for our volunteer fire department? We can always use more people."

"No, but I certainly appreciate all that you guys do for our community. I am hoping that you might be able to help me with something for school. I'm trying to get the students more interested in science by doing experiments and demonstrations, rather than just lecturing to them every day. We are beginning a chapter in our science book on the Big Bang Theory, which is how some people think the universe was created. I want the kids to see for themselves that this theory really doesn't make sense."

The two firemen had never really questioned the Big Bang Theory. It never seemed like a big deal, but they were excited at the possibility of doing something different. Frank quickly replied, "We'd love to help. Things around here are pretty boring most of the time. What can we do?"

Ben explained, "I would like to set off a large fire cracker or cherry bomb that is surrounded by a sphere of objects, like small rubber balls or something that won't damage anything -- something that will show visibly the outward motion of the objects when the fire cracker explodes. Can you come up with something that might work? I want the students to understand that a big explosion only causes objects to fly away from the blast and that the objects don't start to orbit each other like our solar system."

Frank and Jim were getting more excited about helping and started to brainstorm some ideas. Ben said, "Since it is not legal for me to set off fireworks, would it be possible for you guys to come to school and do that? You will probably need to bring a fire truck just in case. I plan to do this on the football field, which is quite a ways from the school, so there shouldn't be any problems. Before we can do this, I will need to get permission from the Principal, but I wanted to find out if you could help before I approached him."

"Count us in. Just let us know the day and time."

Ben thanked them for their helpfulness and got their phone numbers so he could stay in touch. Since it was Saturday, Ben didn't know if Mr. Reed would be in his office at school or not, but he decided to drive by the school and check. Sure enough, his car was in the parking lot. In fact it was the only car in the parking lot. Ben had noticed that most teachers didn't put in any more time at school than was necessary, so he was a bit surprised to find the Principal's car there.

Ben entered the school and headed toward Mr. Reed's office. Before he got there, Mr. Reed exploded through his door and started walking hurriedly down the hallway toward the exit, not even noticing Ben. Ben quickly spoke, "Good morning, Mr. Reed."

"Oh, Mr. Harper, I'm surprised to see you here on a nice morning like this," Mr. Reed replied.

"Actually, Mr. Reed, I wanted to talk to you about something regarding my science class."

"I'm in a bit of a hurry this morning. Can't this wait till some other time?"

Ben replied, "I'm trying to make arrangements for a class demonstration this week. I would like to have the fire department come to the football field on Wednesday and set off a fire cracker to demonstrate a principle that we are learning in the next chapter in our book. I wanted ..."

Obviously Mr. Reed was in a rush to get going and he interrupted Ben before he could finish his explanation. "Mr. Harper, I don't care what you do as long as it is legal, safe, and doesn't cost the school anything. OK?"

"I'm good with all those things. Thanks. I may have a few more things in the coming weeks," Ben said.

"Whatever," Mr. Reed gruffly responded. "The same criteria apply. I've got to go."

In amazement Ben replied, "Thanks, Mr. Reed. Have a good weekend." Ben had prepared himself for a much harder sell. He couldn't believe that the Principal had just agreed to his requests without a more detailed explanation and without even putting up an argument.

Ben quickly called Frank and Jim at the fire station and told them he received approval to proceed. Ben set up the demonstration for the upcoming Wednesday. That would give him time to lead into the subject and also give the firemen some time to get things organized.

Chapter 9

On Monday Ben told his class to open their books to Chapter 4, Creation of the Universe. The chapter was almost exclusively on the Big Bang Theory. Ben's goal was to get the kids to question the logic behind the theory and somehow move the discussion into the direction that only a divine force, God himself, could have created the universe and life on planet earth. He knew he had to be careful how he handled any discussion of this nature, since he was strictly forbidden from talking about God in school. But, somehow he knew that if God could create the universe, then coordinating a mere conversation about the true nature of creation shouldn't be a big problem.

"OK, class, before you read this chapter, what do you know about the Big Bang Theory?"

"That's how the universe was created," Pete said. "Initially there was nothing and then suddenly there was a big explosion of super dense material in space. The explosion caused giant particles to be blown out into space. These particles are the stars and planets."

Ben said, "That sounds like a pretty good summary. Let's talk about the word theory. What is it?"

Becky replied, "A theory is what people think happened."

"A guess based on good probability," Jim said.

Ben interjected, "I looked up the definition in the dictionary and here is what I found, 'An Idea that is suggested or presented as possibly true but that is not known or proven to be true.' So, Becky is correct, it is merely what people think may have happened. It is an idea, not a proven fact. Please keep this in mind as we go through this section."

After more discussion, it was time for class to end. Ben said, "Please read Chapter 4 for tomorrow and we will discuss this further. On Wednesday we will meet on the football field for a demonstration." Ben noticed that that comment seemed to generate some excitement. Something to look forward to – that is always good, he thought. "So don't plan to be sick on Wednesday. You won't want to miss this! Does someone have a video camera that we can use to tape the demonstration, one that will play slow motion?"

Pete raised his hand. "I have one I can bring."

"Good, I will see you all tomorrow."

On Tuesday Ben began, "I hope you all spent some time reading the chapter. Assuming you have, what does the book say are the basic thoughts behind the Big Bang Theory?"

The class voiced the following ideas as Ben wrote them on the board:

"The universe all began as a super dense, super hot mass somewhere in empty space."

"No one seems to know where or how this dense mass began."

"A sudden explosion or expansion took place causing the dense mass to radiate particles outward."

"As the particles cooled, they formed stars, moons, and planets."

"It all happened about 13.7 billion years ago."

"The universe is still expanding."

"Because the universe is expanding, people think it must have begun as a single mass."

"OK", Ben said. "I can tell that you have read the chapter. That is good. In our last class we said that the Big Bang is a theory –

it's what people think happened, but it has not been proven. So, of these ideas that I've written on the board, which ones have actually been proven?"

Holly replied, "Scientists have proven that the universe is still expanding."

"Good, Holly", Ben said. "What about the others?"

Paul said, "I can't find in the book where anyone has been able to verify any of the others. It is merely their best guess."

"Since only one thing can be verified, then we need to think about how logical this theory really is," Ben said. "OK, our class is over for today, but remember that tomorrow we will meet on the football field for our demonstration. Pete, please remember to bring your video camera. See you all tomorrow."

Ben was both nervous and excited as he drove to school on Wednesday. He really wanted this demonstration to be successful – in several ways. He wanted the kids to become more enthused about science and school in general by doing things a bit "outside the box." He wanted them to think logically for themselves – to realize that they are capable of far more than what they think. He wanted this demonstration to generate hope – hope of something exciting for today and even for the future beyond today. Sometimes hope is more of a motivator than the event itself.

Frank and Jim arrived at 9:00 a.m. with their fire truck to get things set up for the demonstration at 10:00. Fortunately, Ben did not have a 9:00 class, so he could go out and help them and to make sure they were all on the same page with what was planned. The fire truck was merely a precautionary measure, but it certainly generated some excitement in the school. Many of the classrooms had windows facing the football field, so when the truck pulled up there were a lot of curious on-lookers.

Frank and Jim had experimented with several prototype materials prior to Wednesday to see which would generate the most desired effect. Their end result was a one foot cube made of plaster of Paris with a cherry bomb cast in the center. It was configured with a long fuse so that it could be ignited from a safe distance. The cube was suspended from the cross bar on the goal post at one end of the football field. Ben wanted it to be suspended to simulate the theoretical condition in space.

The students arrived promptly and were very eager to see what Ben had arranged. They were surprised to see the fire truck and the firemen, having no idea what was planned. Ben explained, "The purpose of this demonstration this morning is to simulate, on a tremendously smaller scale, what the Big Bang may have looked like. These firemen, Frank and Jim, are going to conduct this experiment for us, since it is a little dangerous. So please follow their instructions very carefully. They have made a cube, which is meant to simulate the super dense material that supposedly existed in the beginning before the universe was formed. Inside the cube is a large fire cracker. Frank and Jim are going to light the fuse so that we can observe what happens to the cube. I want Pete to record the explosion with his video camera so that we can review this in class and analyze what happens during the explosion."

Then Ben turned to the firemen and asked, "Frank and Jim, can you brief us on any safety measures we should follow?"

Jim was prepared for this question. "First, we would like everyone to put on these safety glasses that we brought. Second, we want everyone to stand about 100 feet away. We've conducted trial runs with this experiment and it appears that 100 feet should be a safe distance to avoid any flying material. And third, please watch for any stray sparks that may ignite the grass. The grass is very green right now, so we don't expect any problems. We brought the fire truck with some water, just in case. So if you see any sparks or smoldering grass, please yell out to us. Otherwise, I think we are ready to begin. Once we set the fuse, it will take about 10 seconds before the fire cracker goes off. That will give Frank and me enough time to move safely away."

"Great," Ben said. "Now let's all move back to about the 30 yard line. Pete, please set up your camera so that you can get a good angle on the cube."

When everyone was safely in place, and Pete had his camera rolling, Ben gave the signal for the firemen to proceed. Frank lit the fuse and then ran back to the fire truck to join Jim. Ten seconds seemed like forever, but everyone could see the flame slowly burning up to the cube. Once the flame reached the cube, there was nothing. It was like the fuse stopped burning. Ben heard a few snickers from the students and was beginning to think that maybe the experiment had failed. But then there was a deafening explosion! It was considerably louder than what Ben had expected, and he could feel the shock wave as it resonated through his body. He suddenly hoped that he hadn't made a bad decision for trying this experiment. Obviously, the entire school heard the explosion, including Mr. Reed. His stomach began to feel uneasy, but he tried to suppress his fears as he re-grouped his students.

Ben learned after the explosion that Frank and Jim had warned the police about what was taking place, in case they received any call. Fortunately, the football field was quite a ways from the school, which helped to retard the noise somewhat. Ben was also glad he had previously alerted all of the teachers about the experiment so that someone wouldn't call in a bomb threat. Ben later learned that Mr. Reed had been out of town for a conference on the day of the experiment – a great blessing, Ben thought. Otherwise, he was sure he would have been making an unpleasant trip to Mr. Reed's office.

The students were all excited following the experiment and were talking non-stop. Once Ben got their attention, he asked, "Before we pick up all the pieces, I want you to walk around and take notes on what you see. Pay attention to the size of the pieces, shape of the pieces, distance from the explosion, and anything that might help us as we analyze this in class tomorrow."

Ben had also brought a camera and asked one of the students to take pictures of the objects. "Pretend like you are detectives evaluating a crime scene. Collect all of the evidence you can. Once you've finished looking at the site, please pick up all of the pieces and put them in this cardboard box."

Ben went over and talked to Frank and Jim. "I'm really grateful for all your help on this. You guys did an excellent job and I'm hopeful students will have a good learning experience from all of this."

Frank replied, "Thanks for asking us, Ben. We enjoyed the excitement. If you ever need anything else, just let us know. If any of your students would like to tour the fire house, we'd be happy to show them around. We're always looking for new recruits."

Ben thanked them again. "Thanks guys. It has been great working with you and I know the students were impressed. I will certainly announce your offer to them in class."

Chapter 10

In class the next day the students were buzzing with comments. "That was awesome!" "No one else has ever done anything like this before in science class!" "How did you get Mr. Reed to agree to this?"

Ben finally got the class settled down and then began. "First I want to say that we owe Frank and Jim, our firemen, a big thank you for making this experiment possible. If you get a chance, please thank them for all of their effort. They also told me that you are all welcome anytime to go and visit the firehouse for a tour. I encourage you to take them up on their offer. Fire fighting is part of science also.

"So," Ben continued, "Our mission yesterday was to observe the simulation of the Big Bang Theory and to collect evidence to help us understand what happens when an object explodes. Let's first talk about what you saw and what you found when you looked for the pieces. What were some things you observed?"

The students eagerly chimed in: "The block broke up into thousands of pieces." "The pieces flew in all directions from the center of the explosion." "The block broke up into pieces of all sizes." "The pieces were irregularly shaped." "Some of the pieces were big and some were very small."

Those are all excellent observations," Ben said. "Let's also watch Pete's video to see if we can learn anything else. Pete, go ahead and play your video at regular speed. Notice that because it happens so fast, about all we can see is a large cloud of dust. Now, Pete, play it again but in slow motion."

Pete reset the machine and played it again at a very slow speed. "Now," Ben said, "What do you see this time?"

The students replied: "A sudden burst of energy." "Fragments flying outward in straight lines in all directions." "No fragments remaining at the center of the blast." "All of the fragments were of the same composition."

Ben continued, "Let's compare what we learned with the Big Bang Theory. Did you observe anything that is inconsistent with the Theory?"

"All of the suns, moons, and planets are typically spherical. I didn't see any spheres in the fragments that we picked up," Jimmy said.

"Yeah," Tammy said, "and I didn't see any objects orbiting other objects like we see in our solar system."

Ben built upon that thought by saying, "We should also note that the earth rotates on a very precise schedule every day – one rotation every 24 hours and the earth orbits the sun on a very precise schedule – one orbit every 365 days. All of the other planets have their own precise schedules. Then we have the moon that rotates around the earth on a precise schedule. We didn't see any of these things happening when we conducted our experiment. So, what are we concluding?"

John replied, "I think we're saying the Big Bang Theory doesn't support what we know is true in our universe."

"If that is true," Amanda said, "then why do so many people accept the Big Bang Theory?"

Ben tried to direct the discussion. "People inherently want to believe in something. They need some kind of an explanation that defines the unknown."

"But," Buck said, "if people want to hold onto something and the Big Bang Theory isn't true, then they are holding onto the wrong thing."

Ben replied, "You are exactly right, Buck. People often accept what they don't understand, because it seems to provide answers."

Anne suddenly spoke up. "I believe we already have the answer, but most people don't acknowledge it."

"And what is that?" Ben asked.

"The Bible tells us that God created the universe and all living things. He did it in seven days, not millions of years. With the great diversity in the universe, it is the only explanation that makes sense."

Ben, amazed at the boldness of this normally shy student, said, "I have to be very careful what I say as a teacher. The school has imposed restrictions on what we can teach regarding the divine nature of creation that Anne has described. As students, you do not have such restrictions, so you are free to state your thoughts and ask questions freely. I will try to respond to your comments and questions discretely, since I really don't want to lose my job. I totally agree with Anne's statement. The characteristics of the universe; its great complexity, diversity, and order are beyond any type of explosion that could have occurred."

Alex raised his hand and said, "Scientists have estimated the universe to be millions of years old, but if God created it in seven days and immediately put man on earth, then the universe probably isn't nearly as old as scientists believe. How can you explain that huge difference?"

"What if, when the earth was created, it was created as a mature planet?" Ben said. "The first people on earth could not have been infants, or there would not have been anyone to care for them. The first animals could not have been babies or they would not have survived. Likewise, what if the universe was created in a mature state, like it had been there for millions of years, but in reality it was brand new? I believe that scientists are often deceived by not realizing this basic fact."

Buck said, "Yeah, but can you prove that?"

"Can you disprove it? We were able to disprove the Big Bang Theory with a simple experiment, but no one has been able to disprove the creation story."

The period came to a close, and the students went on to their next class. Ben hoped their experiment and discussion about the creation of the universe might start them thinking about God and His sovereignty.

Chapter 11

The next chapter in the science book was on simple machines. Ben really wanted to build on the energy that was generated by his explosion experiment. He had an idea but needed the help of one of the smaller students in class. Ben decided to talk to Anne to see if she would agree to help with another demonstration. Anne was only about 4' 10" tall and weighed less than 100 pounds. Anne was normally very quiet; however, her boldness in talking about God and creation had impressed him. He had noticed that several students often picked on her, Buck being one of them. But in her quiet demeanor, she never responded to their insults – a quality Ben admired in her.

Ben asked Anne to stay after class the next day so he could explain his plan to her. Ben began, "I don't want to embarrass you by talking to you separately. I've observed that you are different than most of the other students. I mean, different in a good way. Your gentle and quiet spirit[5] as well as your non-response to insults leads me to believe that you are a Christian. I'm probably going out on a limb here, but is that a correct assessment?"

"I am," she said. "I became a believer when I was in junior high. There aren't many Christians in this school, so sometimes it gets hard."

"I encourage you to stand firm[6] in your faith. Someday you will be rewarded. That is a promise given to all believers," Ben said. "The reason I wanted to talk to you is to see if you would be willing to help me with our next science demonstration. This will be the

---

[5] I Peter 3:3-4 – Your beauty should not come from outward adornment, such as elaborate hair styles and the wearing of gold jewelry and fine clothes. Rather, it should be that of your inner self, the unfading beauty of a gentle and quiet spirit, which is of great worth in God's sight. (NIV)
[6] I Peter5:9a – Resist him (Satan), standing firm in the faith ... (NIV)

lead-in to our next chapter. We are going to be studying simple machines, which generate a mechanical advantage. They allow us to do things with less effort. I would like to rig up a block and tackle system to show how a small force can lift a heavy weight."

"So, how can I help?"

"Well, I would like you to demonstrate that you can lift Buck off the floor by pulling the rope on the block and tackle with only one hand."

"But how can I do that? He is more than twice my size!"

"If I can set up a block and tackle with enough ropes, you will only have to pull about 20 pounds, which I am confident you can do. I really have two reasons for doing this demonstration: one is to teach everyone how simple machines make life easier for us, and the second is to improve Buck's respect for other people. He has come a long way since class began, but his attitude still has some rough edges. I think with this demonstration we may have a chance to change his character."

"How do you plan to do that?"

"If you are willing to pull the rope, I'll take care of the rest. Obviously, there is no guarantee, but I think it is worth a try."

"OK," Anne said. "But I'm not out to embarrass him or create any problems."

"I fully understand. Thank you for your willingness to help."

After school Ben made a quick trip to the local hardware store to see if he could get some supplies for the demonstration. Fortunately, Ben encountered the owner soon after he entered. Ben explained what he wanted to do – to rig up a pulley system with enough rope to lift a platform with someone standing on it. The owner graciously volunteered to loan Ben the pulleys and rope so he wouldn't have to spend his own money for a short term experiment. Ben merely had to return the items when he was finished. Ben was thrilled. He hadn't expected such a generous offer. Ben loaded up the items and headed for home. To get everything ready, he had some assembly work to complete.

In class the next day, Ben finished the last topic and for the last few minutes explained his upcoming game plan. "Tomorrow we will be performing a demonstration in the gym, but in order to do this I need two people to help. First, I need someone that is big and strong."

All eyes turned to Buck, since he was by far the biggest kid in the class. Buck quickly responded to the sudden moment of glory. "Here I am. I'm your man."

"Are you sure, Buck? I don't want you to volunteer for something you might not be able to handle," Ben said.

"Mr. Harper, I'm obviously the biggest and strongest person in the class, probably in the school! I can handle it, trust me."

"OK", Ben said. "Does the class agree that Buck is the best candidate?"

"Yeah, Buck is our guy", the class responded. "He can do it!"

Ben was pleased. So far his plan was working. He wanted Buck to volunteer, rather than any other student. He had a feeling that it wouldn't be a problem – he was right. Buck had jumped on the bait! Ben continued, "For the second person, I need someone that is much smaller. I would like to have Anne help, if that is OK with you, Anne?"

She shook her head in agreement. "Good," Ben said. "We should be set then. Tomorrow for our demonstration Anne is going to lift Buck off the floor with one hand! It's not magic. It is just natural strength!"

That comment generated a lot of laughs from the class. Buck, unaware that Ben had planned this event said, "No way. She can't lift me even with both hands. She can't lift me with both hands and both feet! That is impossible. I'm at least twice her size!"

Calmly Ben said, "Buck, are you saying you are not willing to participate? I'm sure I can find someone else."

Not wanting to be embarrassed in front of the class by a feather weight female, Buck said, "Yeah, I'll do it. There is no way she can do that. Not with me!"

"Good," Ben said, "then I think we're all set. Please show up at the gym for our class tomorrow rather than come here. Oh, Buck, just for the record, how much do you weigh?"

Buck proudly responded, "220 pounds, and it is all muscle!"

Somehow Ben doubted that, but he got the information that he needed – Buck's weight. So far everything with Buck had gone just the way Ben had expected. He had been confident that Buck's ego and macho attitude would cause him to accept the challenge.

After school, Ben assembled his multi-pulley block and tackle system so that the force needed to lift Buck would only be about 20 pounds. He was sure Anne could pull that much with one hand. He also built a wooden platform for Buck to stand on and connected it by ropes to the end of the block and tackle. He had arranged with the janitor at school to help him hang the block and tackle from a beam running across the gym. The beam was high enough to suspend the pulleys above the platform as it sat on the floor.

Ben met the janitor early the next morning to get everything set up. Fortunately there were no gym classes prior to Ben's science class, so no one would be able to see or mess with his set-up prior to class time. Just for peace of mind after everything was arranged, Ben had the janitor stand on the platform while he pulled the rope. It worked perfectly. The multi-pulley system allowed Ben to easily lift the janitor a couple inches off the floor while only exerting a small force on the rope. He was confident that little Anne would not have any problem lifting Buck.

All of the students arrived wondering what was going to happen. Anne arrived a few minutes before Buck, which worked out well. It gave Ben a chance to explain how the system was set up and which rope she needed to pull. Anne reacted, "Are you sure this is going to work? If it doesn't, I'll be the laughing stock of the whole school!"

Ben said, "Trust me. I've tried it out with the janitor and it worked really well."

"OK," she said with some hesitation.

Buck arrived intentionally a couple minutes late to add to the drama. He proudly displayed his new T-shirt which had imprinted on it "Big Buck". The kids all cheered as he entered. Ben hadn't counted on that, but it also played well into his plan.

Once the students were seated on the bleachers, Ben called Buck forward and asked him to stand on the platform.

"What is this contraption?" Buck asked with a look of uncertainty on his face. I thought Anne was supposed to lift me with one hand?"

"She will," Ben continued. "The new chapter in our book is on simple machines. This pulley system illustrates one type of simple machine. Now, if I could have Anne come forward. She is merely going to pull this rope with one hand and raise Buck off the floor. Some of the class members started cheering for Buck, while others were cheering for Anne. Everyone was getting into Ben's little experiment. As the drama continued, Ben said, "Go ahead and pull the rope, Anne."

With very little effort Anne was able to lift Buck a few inches off the floor. With that the students cheering for Anne broke out in loud applause. "Little Anne defeats Big Buck". Buck, however, looked a little sheepish. He hadn't anticipated that Mr. Harper had a machine in the plan.

After the demonstration, Anne quietly walked over to Buck and with compassion shook his hand. In a quiet voice that only Ben could hear, Anne said to Buck. "Buck, I know that you are a very strong person, and I believe that God has a purpose for your life. Let Him lead you. Nothing is impossible with God.[7]"

Buck was speechless as he walked over to the rest of the students. He could hear them snickering, "Boy, she got you Buck!" "How could you let little Anne out do you?" "Are you going to get even, Buck?"

At this moment Buck was lost in thought. He realized that Anne had no intention of embarrassing him or putting him down. She seemed to be forgiving him for all his past comments against her. How could she do that? What did she mean "God had a purpose for his life" and "Nothing is impossible with God?" Her attitude and her words were having an impact on him now – how, he wasn't sure, but something was changing.

Back in the classroom the next day Ben explained "Pulleys are a simple machine that gave Anne a mechanical advantage. Mechanical advantage reduces the force required to move objects that weigh considerably more. So, if Buck weighs 220 pounds and Anne lifted him with approximately 20 pounds of force, what is the mechanical advantage?"

Pete raised his hand and said, "I think it is 11 -- 220 divided by 20. Is that right?"

Ben said, "That is exactly right. Good job! Simple machines allow us to move heavy objects, but what do we sacrifice?"

---

[7] Luke 1:37 – "For with God nothing will be impossible." (NKJV)

There were several uncertain looks on the students' faces. "When Anne pulled the rope, how far did Buck move?"

"Only a couple inches," Jane said.

"But," Ben replied, "how far did Anne have to move the rope?"

Jane answered, "Close to 2 feet."

"Right," said Ben. "A simple machine reduces the force, but increases the distance."

Throughout the week, Ben described all of the various simple machines. The class seemed to enjoy the hands-on approach Ben had been taking to study various topics. Class participation was good, and everyone now seemed eager to attend science class. Finally, Ben thought, things were improving.

Chapter 12

During one of the pre-class discussion times, Buck raised his hand and said, "Mr. Harper, can we talk about football today?"

Ben tried not to discourage any topic, unless it was totally inappropriate. He didn't figure the girls would be too interested, but rather than stifle suggestions, he said, "Sure Buck, what would you like to discuss?"

Ben assumed it was probably the upcoming college or pro football season, but Ben was wrong. Buck said, "I think it stinks that our school terminated its football program. I know that we haven't had a winning season for a long time, but to take away a good activity like football isn't fair!"

Several other boys and even a couple of the girls echoed the same thought. Ben was caught a bit off guard. "So, since I'm new here, I obviously don't know about Jordan's football history. Can you enlighten me?"

That question began a flood of comments that included nearly all of the students. Buck began, "Mr. Harris was our previous coach. He was the coach for about 10 years. He really didn't want to be the coach, but the school told him he had to do it or else he would lose his teaching job. As a result, he didn't care whether we won or lost. He just put in his time."

Ben was beginning to see a pattern – the previous coach, the Principal, and several other teachers he had come to know. They were all just putting in their time.

"Yeah," Jimmy said, "after we lost every game last year, and the two years before that, Mr. Harris quit. He quit coaching and he quit teaching."

Tommy chimed in. "Then Mr. Reed terminated the entire football program. It is not fair. Why can't we play football like all the other schools around us?"

Buck asked, "Mr. Harper, maybe you could be our coach? I'll bet you played football in high school!"

Ben quickly responded, "Hold on a bit. I did play a little football in high school, but not too much. I played my freshman year and a couple games in my sophomore year. Then I injured my knee. The doctor advised me to quit football to avoid permanent damage. Though I loved football, I didn't want to quit. But I had to make a hard decision. As far as being your coach, I don't have any experience coaching, and because I quit playing early I don't think I know enough to be a coach."

"But," Tommy said, "You love football. That is 90% of being a coach."

"I think your percentage is a bit exaggerated!" Ben replied.

"Come on, Mr. Harper, please be our coach. You'd be great! I know you would," pleaded Buck.

"We've gone way past our allotted discussion time," Ben said. "We need to get into our lesson. I will think about your request, but at this point I'm not making any commitments plus it sounds like the school has already determined to not have a football program this year – that could be a problem."

Over the weekend, Ben pondered the thought of being a football coach. He had come to Jordan to teach, not to coach. None of the school administrators had even mentioned this to him. He had a feeling there might be more to the story than what the boys had told him in class.

Ben had started attending the local Christian church, where Ruth attended. The people there were extremely friendly and from the beginning made Ben feel right at home. After the service on Sunday, he saw Ruth in the foyer. She came over and greeted him warmly with her always encouraging smile. She asked, "How did things go at school this week, Ben?"

"Things are going fine, except for a new dilemma that came up on Friday."

"And what dilemma is that, Ben?" Ruth inquired with genuine interest.

"Well," Ben said, "during our pre-class discussion time some of the boys expressed their strong desire to play football."

Ruth said, "That sounds like a good thing. What is the dilemma?"

Ben explained, "They want me to be their coach. I played a little football in high school, but not much because of a knee injury. I really don't feel qualified to be a coach."

Ruth in her quiet thoughtful way said, "Perhaps God is showing you a new way to make a difference in the lives of your students. The 12 disciples weren't qualified either when they began the work Jesus called them to do, but look what they accomplished. They spread the Gospel throughout the world!"

"Yeah, but they walked with Jesus every day," Ben rebutted.

"So do you, Ben", Ruth reminded him.

"But there is one other problem. Apparently the football program was terminated by the school at the end of last season. If the program has been terminated, then even if I were willing to be a coach, it doesn't matter."

"It sounds like God is opening a door with your students' request. I think the least you could do is follow up with the Principal and find out the whole story. If God closes that door, then maybe a football team isn't meant to be. But, I would encourage you to pray and have faith. Faith can move mountains[8]".

Ben did pray fervently throughout the remainder of the day for God's direction and he felt at peace being confident that God would accomplish His will.

---

[8] Mt. 17:20 - ... "Truly I tell you, if you have faith as small as a mustard seed, you can say to this mountain, 'Move from here to there' and it will move. Nothing will be impossible for you." (NIV)

Chapter 13

First thing on Monday morning Ben went to the Secretary's office to set up an appointment with Mr. Reed. The earliest appointment he could get was after school at 4:00 p.m. Ben didn't say anything about the football issue in class on Monday because he wanted to meet with Mr. Reed first. He could see inquisitive looks on the boys' faces, but he intentionally ignored them.

Promptly at 4:00 p.m. Ben entered the Secretary's office and took a seat. He could sense nervousness building in his body as he waited. He didn't like meeting with Mr. Reed, although he had been accommodating with his request for the science demonstration. Finally at 4:10 p.m. Mr. Reed opened his door and motioned for Ben to enter. Ben walked into Mr. Reed's office, which seemed even more cluttered than the last time he was there. Ben could not imagine how he accomplished anything.

"Mr. Harper, what is it today?" Mr. Reed barked.

"Well," Ben began, "some of the boys in my science class would like to play football, but I understand the program was cancelled at the end of last year. Being new here, I obviously don't know all the circumstances, but I was wondering if the program could be re-instated?"

"Here's the deal, Mr. Harper. The football team hasn't won a game in three years – not a single game! The players didn't have any discipline and showed no respect for the coach, or anyone else for that matter. At the end of the year the coach resigned, retired from school in fact. Attendance at football games was poor at best. Only a handful of students showed up and that was only to mock their own team. We didn't gain enough revenue from the concession stand to even make it worthwhile. On top of these 'minor' circumstances, the school has no budget to support a football team. So, the logical decision was to terminate the program. With no coach, no attendance, and no budget it is hard to support an extracurricular activity like this."

Feeling a bit overwhelmed by what he just heard, Ben meekly replied, "I was just thinking of the students and how this might be an encouragement to them, since they had expressed some interest."

To that Mr. Reed replied, "Mr. Harper, if you want to organize a team, be their coach, and do it all with no budget, then go right ahead. I'm not going to stop you. Whatever equipment we have is all there is. We have to keep the football field mowed for PE classes, but you will have to do whatever else is required. We have no funds for travel either, so keep that in mind. If you want to tackle this beast, be my guest. Anything else, Mr. Harper?"

"No, Mr. Reed. I get the picture. Thank you for your time."

As Ben drove home, the thoughts in his mind were bouncing around like a hundred rubber balls. He couldn't decide if God had closed the door or if the door was still open. Sometimes knowing God's will wasn't easy. He teeter tottered back and forth on whether to tell the boys that a football program just wasn't going to happen or to take it one more step and see how many boys might be interested. Ben finally reasoned that if there were not enough interested boys, then it would be clear they would not have any football program.

The next day in class during discussion time Ben announced to the class, "I met with Mr. Reed yesterday about reviving the football program."

Before Ben could continue, the boys anxiously asked, "And what did you find out?"

"Well," Ben told them bluntly, "I was told there are a few minor problems with re-instating football. Apparently, last year's team was not very well disciplined, the team members did not show respect, and attendance was very poor. And on top of these issues there is no budget to support a football program this year. That's the negative side of things. On the brighter side, Mr. Reed said we could have a football team as long as we don't spend any school money, and if I am willing to be the coach."

"Will you do it, Mr. Harper? Will you be our coach?" Buck pleaded.

"I've thought about this a lot recently and there are obviously a lot of hurdles to overcome. But I will commit to taking this to the next step, and that is to find out how many boys in school are actually interested in playing. If there isn't enough interest, then we won't be able to have a team."

"Thanks, Mr. Harper! I know we can get enough guys to make a team," Buck said with great excitement.

"You guys talk to others that might want to play. I will make some posters and hang them up. Let's plan to have a meeting with everyone in this room a week from Friday right after school."

Ben was glad to see the boys so enthused, but he was fearful of the outcome. If there were enough boys to have a team, he was fearful of being a coach. He felt totally inadequate for a task like this. On the other hand, if there wasn't enough interest he was fearful that the boys would be really depressed. He didn't want to see that either, especially since they had come so far since the beginning of school.

The next day Ben made a few posters and hung them in some prominent places around school. He really had no idea what to expect. He knew a lot of the boys because of his science classes, but there were many that weren't in any of his classes. As he hung the posters, Ben said a quiet prayer, "Lord, this is in your hands. May your will be done."

Chapter 14

Ben's goal in teaching was to bring honor and glory to God. As he thought about the upcoming meeting, he felt convicted to somehow convey this purpose to all of the football players. He reasoned that if he could teach them to honor God on the football field, then the carryover would be to honor God in every aspect of their lives. Ben realized this was a tough mission, especially since he was forbidden to talk about God on school property. Ben thought, "This is just another detail God will have to work out!"

Ben decided that it would be good to present a list of rules to all the boys on Friday so that they would know ahead of time what he expected. He wanted the rules to reflect God's commands, but he couldn't identify them as coming from the Bible. He suddenly felt that he was on an impossible mission, one that he certainly had not expected, but one that was starting to grow on him.

He thought and prayed a lot throughout the week and finally came up with a list of 10 rules that he felt captured the essence of God's commandments that not only applied to playing football but also applied to all of life. He made numerous copies so that he could hand them out at the meeting.

Buck and the other boys assured him throughout the week that a lot of guys were interested and would be attending the meeting. Ben hoped that all the boys were coming because they were sincere in their desire to play and not just seeking to mock the new coach, potential coach that is.

When Friday classes dismissed, it wasn't long until boys started filing into Ben's room. He could feel his anxiety level increasing, so he silently prayed for God to give him peace. Soon, to Ben's amazement, the room was full of boys, probably 35 at least, freshmen to seniors. Ben was glad to see such a good turnout. He felt encouraged, at least for the moment.

It was time to start, so Ben introduced himself. "My name is Mr. Harper. Some of you know me from science class. I'm a new teacher here at Jordan High. I previously came from Cleveland, Ohio, where I also taught science."

"I'll bet Cleveland wasn't like Jordan!" someone joked.

Ben ignored the comment and continued. "Some of the boys in my science class have expressed interest in having a football team this year. I have learned that the football program was terminated at the end of last year for various reasons."

"Yeah, a perfect 0 and 9 season for three years in a row!" another student blurted out.

"Well," Ben said, "regardless of the reasons, I have approached Mr. Reed and he has sort of given his OK with a few stipulations. I won't go into the stipulations now. The main purpose for this meeting is to determine if there are enough serious players to make a team."

Someone proclaimed, "The room is full, isn't it? That should be plenty for a team."

"On the surface, that would appear to be true," Ben said, "but there are a lot of reasons for wanting to be on a football team, and I'm sure you each have your own. But, if I'm going to be the coach, then our main reason for playing football is to live by a higher standard."

"What kind of reason is that?" someone asked.

"My philosophy is that whatever we do, we should do it to the best of our ability – to a higher standard than the rest of the world. Football teaches you how to live life, not just how to run plays and score points."

Buck really wanted to play football, but he wasn't sure what Mr. Harper was doing. In a more serious tone than Ben had previously heard from Buck, Buck asked, "Mr. Harper, how are we supposed to live by a higher standard?"

"That is an excellent question, Buck. I'm glad you asked. I've prepared a list of 10 rules that I am asking every player to obey. I'm going to hand these out, and then I will review each of them so that you understand what I'm talking about."

"So here are the rules, which apply off the field as well as on the field.

Rule #1 – I will be a man of integrity. That means that you will be honest, you will be trustworthy, and you will stand firm for what is right. No lying, cheating, or immoral activity.

Rule #2 – I will encourage others. Everyone likes to be encouraged whether teammates or classmates. Everyone performs better when they are encouraged, and everyone has a better outlook. People feel valuable when they are encouraged.

Rule #3 – I will bear others' burdens. You will help people whenever they need help, as long as you are able to do so. This applies to family members, fellow students, your teammates, and even strangers. Some burdens are too great for a person to handle by himself. But with the help of others, the burden becomes lighter, easier to bear.

Rule #4 – I will not speak unwholesome words. This includes no profanity, no crude jokes, no racial comments, no arguing, and no complaining.

Rule #5 – I will work hard. Obviously Jordan has not experienced a winning record for some time, so it is going to take hard work to gain victory. But hard work doesn't just apply to football. It applies to school, your job, to your chores at home – pretty much whatever you do. I understand that the school requires every player, regardless of the sport, to maintain a passing grade in every subject to be eligible to play. I take that to mean a 'D' or higher. But since our goal is to live to a higher standard, I'm requiring that every player on this football team maintain a 'C' or higher in every class every week. Maintaining good grades will pay big dividends in your lives whether you opt to go to college or start working.

Rule #6 – I will love my enemies. Obviously we can all love people we like. But the one true test of character is whether you can love your enemies. We think of our opponents as the enemy. In reality they are people just like us. They may say things and do things that make us angry. But there are usually reasons why they act or respond as they do, reasons that we may understand. Our goal is to help them, and not to further the conflict. So, on the football field, for example, if one of the opposing players gets injured, what should you do? Shout arrogantly in his face, 'Ha, you got what you deserved.' No, you should quietly comfort him until his coach can get to him. This is only an example. There are lots of things we can do to love our enemies. Another interesting thing about this Rule is that often when you love your enemy, they are no longer an enemy.

Rule #7 – I will endure insults without retaliation. Many of you I would guess have been the recipients of derogatory comments from upper classmen, from bullies, and sometimes even from parents. As we attempt to field a football team most opponents will be verbally insulting you to mess with your mind – to get your focus off the game. If you let it get to you, it will be very effective. You will want revenge more than victory. We are not going to play with that mentality.

Rule #8 – I will not pollute my body. Anything that causes your mind or body to deteriorate is pollution. This Rule includes no drinking, no smoking, no drugs, no pornography, and no sex (unless you are married and I don't think anyone here falls into that category). Besides being illegal for boys your age, none of these things are healthy in the life of a football player nor are they healthy for anyone living life. All of these things prevent you from living to a higher standard.

Rule #9 – I will be a team player. Life is all about team work. Football is about team work. It takes every player doing his job for a team to be successful. If you think of yourself as better than others or more important than others, then you are being selfish and the team will suffer. Think of others as more important that yourself.

Rule #10 – I will enjoy life. Life is a gift. Enjoy life and don't waste it. Being on a football team is a special privilege. Enjoy it and don't waste it.

"If it all works out for us to have a football team this year, I want to let you know up front that my goal in coaching will not be to train players for a season, but to train men for life. If you can play football according to these rules, then you can also live life according to these rules. I want each of you to take this sheet home and think seriously about what I have just said. If you want to play football you have to commit to these rules. That will be my policy as your coach. We will have another meeting on Monday immediately after school for all of you that want to play. We will then decide how to proceed. I think that is all I have to say. Are there any questions or comments?"

Buck interjected, "Mr. Harper, this is pretty tough stuff!"

Ben said, "I understand football players are pretty tough guys!"

Another student who Ben didn't recognize said, "A 'C' average is hard to get for a lot of us. I don't think we can do it."

Ben replied, "How much do you want to play football? Maybe you just haven't set your goals high enough. You might be surprised what you can accomplish if you set your mind to it. Anything else? If not, I hope to see all of you back here after school on Monday."

Ben could hear a lot of mumbling as the boys left the room. He knew this was going to be a hard thing for them. This approach was probably different than what previous coaches had taken, but Ben's motivation was more than likely different than previous coaches. At this point Ben knew the outcome was in God's hands.

Chapter 15

Over the weekend Ben's mind was flooded with thoughts. Did he go too far with the list of rules? Would enough boys respond to even have a team? Was he knowledgeable enough to even coach football? How could he convey God's truth to these boys without being allowed to talk about God? Finally, Ben took a deep breath and prayed to God, "It is not clear to me what your will is in all of this. I am willing to do whatever you want me to do. Please direct me in the way you want me to go." Ben suddenly felt more relaxed. His next step was to wait and see what Monday brought.

After his last class on Monday, Ben had a free period. He tried to grade papers, but he was having a hard time focusing. He had no idea what to expect, how many kids would show up, or if any would show up. Maybe playing by the rules was more of a commitment than they wanted to make. The minutes seemed to drag on until the bell finally rang. Ben put away his papers and waited patiently for the boys to come. A few filed into the room in the next few minutes, but there was no big crowd as there had been on Friday. Ben waited about ten minutes and then shut the door. Only twelve boys had returned!

Ben thought, "It takes eleven players on the field at all times. How can we play an entire season with only twelve?" He reasoned that this was God's signal that the door had been closed. He had tried, but the lack of commitment was the deciding factor. They would have to forego a football team for another year.

Ben was just ready to verbalize his thoughts, when Buck spoke up. "Mr. Harper, I know that we only have twelve boys in this room, but we have all seriously thought about your 10 rules and we are committed to doing our best to follow them. I'm sure we will mess up, but if you will help us, we really want to continue with the football team, even with only twelve players. I'm not necessarily a religious person, but I had a very wise girl tell me once that 'with God anything is possible.'"

Ben knew that Buck was referring to the science demonstration in the gym when Anne lifted him off the floor with the block and tackle. He was impressed that Buck had retained that thought. Perhaps God was working in his life.

"What do the rest of you boys think?" Ben asked.

Without hesitation they all echoed Buck's comments. Ben said, "If we are going to play competitively, it is going to take a lot of hard work. Most teams switch players on offense and defense, so they have a chance to rest before they get back on the field. You won't have that luxury. You'll have to play offense, defense, and special teams without resting. In addition you will have to help chalk the field before games and carry equipment in and out before and after games, since there are no funds for others to help with this. We will also have to make our own vehicle arrangements for out of town games. On top of all this, I want to emphasize again that I've never coached before."

Ben tried to mention all the negatives he could think of because he could only imagine how difficult it would be with only twelve players. Then Buck said, "Mr. Harper, we believe in you. Do you believe in us?"

This was like a trick question. If he said no, he would lose all rapport that he was working so hard to establish. If he said yes, he was making a commitment to something he wasn't sure he could do. He knew he couldn't let them down. "Yes, I believe in you. I think you are capable of moving mountains!"

"All right!" Buck exclaimed. "We've got ourselves a football team!" Everyone cheered.

It was a happy moment for the boys, but Ben knew the road was going to be difficult for them -- and for him as well. They agreed to meet again tomorrow after school to check on the status of uniforms, pads, and other equipment.

Ben saw Ruth in her front yard tending her flowers as he was driving home from school. He decided to stop and say hi. As usual her smile was her greeting card. They talked a few minutes and then he mentioned the football team situation. "Well," Ben said, "I took your advice and met with Mr. Reed. He sure has a gnarly attitude about things! Anyway, the bottom line is that he will allow us to have a football team, but there is no money available for expenses that might be incurred. We would have to provide our own travel, we would have to take care of all field preparations, and we would not be able to purchase any new equipment."

"So, what did you decide to do?"

"I took the next step to see how many boys might be interested," Ben said. "I held an informational meeting last Friday and about 35 boys attended.

"Wow that sounds like a lot of boys want to play football!" Ruth exclaimed.

"Prior to the meeting I developed a list of 10 rules, rules that I felt were critical to not just football, but to life. I passed the rules out at the meeting and discussed them with the boys. I told them they would have to commit to these rules if they wanted to play on the team. We met again today after school. Only twelve boys showed up."

"What were the rules?" Ruth asked. "Sounds like you certainly weeded out the group."

Ben pulled a copy from his brief case and handed it to her. She took a few minutes and read through the list. "Ben," she said, "these are all from the Bible."

"Yes, I know. I felt if God was calling me to be a coach, then it must be for reasons more than just coaching a football team. I want to be able to convey God's standards to the boys so that they will be equipped to live life in a way that honors God."

"Can you have a team with only twelve players?" Ruth asked.

"Well, it takes eleven to make a team, so we would only have one substitute. Most schools have 30 to 40 players, so they can rotate throughout the game. Playing with only twelve will be tough on the players. I'm not sure they realize that."

"So, what are you going to do?"

"The boys really want to do it, so as it stands now, we are going to try it. I really feel handicapped, though, not being able to talk to the boys about God when implementing these rules. If only I had the freedom to do that."

Ruth thought for a moment and then said, "I have an idea that may help you in that regard. When the school was originally built back in the early 50's, the school district purchased the land from Fred Dawson. Due to budget issues, they did not have enough money to purchase land for the football field. Fred ultimately worked out a long term lease so the school could use the property for a football field and also for the Bus Garage. Fred passed away quite a few years ago, but his son, Roger Dawson, now owns the property. He has continued to lease the property to the school. In fact he is the grounds keeper for the school, and he performs most of the maintenance on the buses. If I remember correctly, the building has a good-sized meeting room, which they occasionally use for meetings with the bus drivers. Ben, if he would let you use the meeting room, you could talk to your players about whatever you wanted, since the property isn't owned by the school. Roger is also a Christian man, so I think there is a good chance he may help you."

"Wow that is certainly food for thought. I've seen Roger mowing grass and trimming bushes around the school, but I've never really talked to him. I think I will have to pay him a visit."

Ben thanked Ruth for the new information and then left for home. He definitely needed to talk to Roger Dawson!

Chapter 16

After school on Tuesday, Buck and some of the other boys showed Ben where the football equipment was stored. There was a small room adjacent to the boys' locker room that was dedicated to sports equipment. One area in particular seemed to be dedicated to football gear. As soon as Ben opened the door, he could tell that last year had not ended on a good note. Everything had been literally thrown into the room. It was just one big pile of stuff. As they started to sort through things, Ben quickly determined that the uniforms were in very poor condition. Most of them had not even been washed after the last game. Grass stains and ground in dirt were common on almost every pair of pants and on almost every jersey. Some of the uniforms were torn and ragged.

"Well," Ben told the boys "see if you can find enough equipment that fits and that isn't in extremely bad condition. Whatever you pick out, please take it home and have it washed. Also, pick out a helmet that fits. Make sure it has all the padding on the inside. I want you to remove all the stickers on the outside." The previous coach had given stickers to put on a player's helmet each time he made a good play. "Clean them up the best you can."

Ben had the boys help him organize the equipment and stack it neatly on the shelves that were in the room. A lot of the equipment was in such poor condition, that Ben had the boys put it in the dumpster. The whole effort was a bit depressing, Ben thought. He had hoped to find things in much better condition. Ben's mind began to wonder, "What kind of journey is God leading us into?" At this point, he knew that only time would reveal the outcome. Before they left the locker room, they all agreed to meet Thursday after school to start practice.

In his free time over the next few days Ben was able to contact the other schools in Jordan's conference to let them know that Jordan would have a team after all. The other schools were happy to hear the news, since otherwise they would have had one week without a game. Ben also spent some time reading the high school rule book, which he deemed necessary if he planned to be a coach. He didn't want to appear too ignorant. In his review of the rules he did find one fact that might prove useful. A team must field at least ten players or they would be forced to forfeit the game. Ben had been concerned that the number was eleven, the standard number for a football team. In case of injury, or who knows what else, at least they could play with as few as ten.

As practice began on Thursday, the boys were all excited. It was something new to anticipate. Ben had observed that hope was a big motivator in any aspect of life. Ben located a four man blocking sled along the end of the Bus Garage. Upon closer inspection, however, Ben realized that the sled was half smashed. It looked like someone had tried to run it over with a four-wheel drive pickup truck. He could only surmise that this was some release of frustration over the last year's losing season. It was certainly beyond repair, so they would merely have to practice without a sled.

Ben had the boys start practice with some calisthenics, some of the ones he could remember from his short time in football. The boys had some others from last year, so they kind of pooled their experiences and came up with what became a fairly regularly routine. As Ben watched, he silently prayed that this year would not be another discouragement to the boys. It was early to tell, but it appeared that there was a variety of abilities on the team. As the team went through their exercise routine, Ben jotted down each player's name. Buck and Tommy were seniors. Sam, Zeke, and Rob were juniors. Pete, Cody, Russ, Corky, and Will were sophomores. Jimmy and Wes were freshmen.

A definite concern was that the team members were not very big. Buck was the biggest player at about 220 pounds, although he was a bit overweight. Ben suspected that daily practices would get the excess weight off in short order. Jimmy was the smallest player at 125 pounds, Ben guessed. Size wise everyone else was in between. Ben estimated the team average at about 175 pounds. Feelings of doubt began to creep into Ben's mind. He was sure that every team in the conference would be bigger, considerably bigger, than Jordan's team.

Then there was the more obvious problem of only having twelve players. Most basketball teams had more players than that on their rosters! Ben didn't even have enough players to scrimmage. How could he make it work with so few team members? What if one or two get injured or couldn't maintain their grades? Then the whole effort would be in vain and they all would be embarrassed. Experience was also a problem. Only Buck and Tommy had any significant experience from last year. The juniors had played some but not much. The sophomores and freshmen had no experience playing varsity football. Ben realized that Satan was putting all of these negative thoughts in his mind. Despite all of the negatives, Ben knew that God had opened several doors for them to even have a team. Why would God back out now? Ben recognized his courage was slipping, until one of his favorite Bible verses came to mind – Joshua 1:9. Ben remembered that God spoke to Joshua when Joshua took over leadership of the Israelites after Moses had passed away. God told Joshua, "I command you, be strong and courageous! Do not be afraid or discouraged. For the Lord your God is with you wherever you go."

The first few practices were a little awkward. With everyone's help Ben was trying to get a routine established. It was coming together, although slowly. There was only three weeks until the first game. Ben knew they had a lot to accomplish, if they were going to be ready. The boys seemed to realize that too, because they were really working hard.

"Good work, guys! You are doing great!" Ben tried to encourage them. They had been working almost entirely on conditioning and basics the first week, the latter especially since most of the players hadn't played much football. With such a lightweight team, Ben knew that blocking was going to be a problem.

Ben offered them some words of insight. "More than likely, we are going to be smaller than most, if not all of our opponents. That means, we must play smart in order to hold our own. If you are playing defense, you have to feel the play as much as see it. If your opponent is trying to push you in one direction, it is probably because they are running the ball the other direction. They will always try to block you away from the play. Therefore, when you feel the direction you are being pushed, try to move quickly in the opposite direction. Sometimes you can duck under the blocker; sometimes you can spin and roll around the blocker. Don't just rely on your eyes to tell you where the ball is.

To practice this I'm going to put a blindfold on the defensive player. An offensive player will try to block you in one direction. I want you to feel which way you are being pushed and then move opposite to that."

Ben ran through the drill several times until each player got the hang of it. "Now," Ben said, "let's assume you are playing offense and we call a play to run between two linemen. You want to block the opponent away from the path of our running back. You want to open a hole for him. Since your opponent will probably be bigger than you, you are going to have to hit quick and hard, and you must stay low.

"But," Russ said, "I don't see how we can block guys that are way bigger than we are."

"Well," Ben replied, "it is a matter of physics. Maybe we can demonstrate this concept. Sam, did you drive your big pickup truck to school today?"

"Yeah, coach, it is in the parking lot."

"Good," Ben said. "Let's all move to the parking lot. I want to show you something. Sam, how much do you think your truck weighs?"

"Probably 4000 pounds, at least."

"OK, I want you to put your truck in neutral.

"Russ, I want you to get behind the truck and try to push it while you are standing straight up."

Russ pushed hard. "Coach, I can't move it."

"Now, stay low and lean forward when you push", Ben responded.

"I can move it!" Russ exclaimed.

"The lower you get the more pushing force you have. If you can move a 4000 pound truck, then a 250 pound lineman should be no problem."

The boys were impressed with the demonstration and realized that they could do more than they thought.

Ben further encouraged them, "If you are moving and your opponent isn't, then you've got momentum on your side. If he starts to overpower you, then take a quick half step back and lunge at his knees. This will hopefully knock him down and give our runner a chance to get passed him. He may fall on top of you, but you will have accomplished your mission. Now let's run through this drill too." After a few attempts, they all seemed to master the technique fairly well.

Ben noticed that Roger Dawson was working near the Bus Garage. Perhaps this would be a good time to talk to him, Ben thought. So, he told the boys to wrap up practice with a few wind sprints. Buck asked, "How many do you want us to run, Coach?"

As Ben started walking toward the Bus Garage, he turned and said, "As many as you think it will take to win!"

Chapter 17

Ben introduced himself to Roger. "Hi, I'm Ben Harper, the new science teacher here at Jordan High."

Roger shook his hand and replied, "And the football coach as well, it appears!"

"Through some unusual circumstances, I somehow ended up being the football coach also."

"Well, God sometimes works in mysterious ways, doesn't He?" Roger commented.

"That He does," Ben replied. Ben was glad to see that Roger appeared to be a Godly man, as Ruth had indicated. "I understand that you actually own the football field as well as the Bus Garage."

"That is right," Roger confirmed. "Our family has maintained a lease agreement with the school ever since the school was built. I help out with maintenance on the buses and upkeep on the grounds. I love being around kids, and this gives me a great opportunity to stay in touch with some of them."

"I love kids too," Ben replied, "and I'm trying to influence them in a Godly way, but the school has a strict policy that teachers and coaches cannot talk about God or spiritual things on school property. Since I'm attempting to work with the football players, and since your Bus Garage is not on school property, I wanted to see if you would permit the team to meet in your conference room on game nights. I could then speak to them without breaking any rules."

Roger's eyes lit up. "That's a great idea. We seldom use the conference room anymore and the room is closer to the field than the locker room in the school. There is a big chalk board on the wall and plenty of chairs. In fact, let me give you a key and you can use the room anytime you want. I'd be happy to chalk the field before games, if that would help. Most of the equipment and lime is here in the garage anyway."

"Wow, I certainly appreciate your kindness and willingness to help. I think we will need all the help we can get!"

Over the next few weeks Ben had the boys practice some simple plays that he had developed. He was also starting to get a feel for where each boy would best fit in the lineup. But, he continually stressed that everybody had to be flexible and able to play multiple positions, if necessary. They really didn't have a good extra point or field goal kicker, so running and passing would have to be their offensive attack. Cody and Rob were excellent runners. They were fast, which would hopefully give Jordan one advantage over the other schools. Zeke, who would probably be the quarterback, was extremely clever with his hands. He could hide the football better than anyone.

Before every practice Ben would review his 10 rules with the boys. He stressed how important the rules were, not just for football, but for living life. One day after reviewing the rules and while they were still on the field, Ben asked, "What is our purpose in having the rules?" There was silence for a moment, as Ben could tell that they were trying to remember.

Then Pete said, "To help us live by a higher standard."

"That is right," Ben said. "And why do we want to live by a higher standard?"

There was silence once again because Ben had not talked about this before. Not because he didn't want to but because when he first presented the rules he was on school property, and he knew that talking about God was forbidden. But they weren't on school property now. They were on the football field. It was time they were given the whole story.

Pete replied, "So we can be better than others?"

"No," Ben said, "that may be what it seems like, but the reason we want to live by a higher standard is to bring honor and glory to God. The Bible teaches that God created us to bring glory to Him[9]. That is our purpose for living. If we don't accomplish that, then we have failed our mission."

Will said, "I think you just made up all of this stuff. If there is a God, He doesn't care what we do."

"Will, all of these rules come straight from the Bible. I didn't make them up. They apply to every aspect of your lives – whether you are playing football, going to school, working at a job, everything. Hopefully, as we go through the season, you will see that God is working in your lives. He wants you to enjoy life, the life that He has given you – Rule 10. "

Practice went well, but no one seemed to say much after Ben's comments.

Ben had a growing concern that the boys' grades were going to be a problem. All of the teachers were required to turn in weekly grades for all students involved in sport activities. Each player had to have passing grades for the previous week, or he was ineligible to play in the current week. With Ben's rules he had raised the bar to "C" grades, not just passing grades.

Ben checked in at the office for last week and found that several of the boys were having difficulty making "C's". With only a couple weeks before the first game, Ben had to make sure everyone would be eligible, especially with only twelve players. The team couldn't afford to have anyone missing.

After practice the next day, he called a quick meeting. "Once you guys get dressed, I want to meet with you in the locker room

---

[9] Rom. 11:36 – For from him and through him and for him are all things. To him be glory forever! (NIV)

for a few minutes." With everyone assembled, Ben began his comments. "One of our standards is that every player maintains a 'C' grade or better in every class. So, we are going to put Rule 3 in to practice – I will bear other's burdens. If you are good in math, then I want you to help your teammate that is struggling in math. Likewise, if you are good in English, then help your teammate that is struggling in English. If we help each other, I'm confident we can get everyone to a 'C' or better in every class. Starting tomorrow we are going to spend 45 minutes after practice helping each other with homework. We will meet in the Bus Garage conference room. There is a big table there as well as a chalk board, if we need it. Any objections to this plan?"

Buck said, "Sounds good to me, coach. We need to have everyone eligible if we are going to have a team. It will be real embarrassing if we have to forfeit a game because we don't have enough players." They all nodded their heads in agreement.

Between preparation for science classes and trying to keep up with everything required for the football team, Ben had been very busy. He was glad for Sunday. It was a chance to go to church and get recharged. With the hecticness of each day, it was easy to lose his focus on what was really important – honoring God in all things. The Sunday message was always helpful and his new friends at church were always an encouragement to him. They were faithfully praying for him and for that he was very grateful.

There were nine games in the season. The first two games were non-conference games because there weren't enough teams in the conference to fill out the entire season. Ben was actually thankful that was the case. A new coach with a small inexperienced team needed a couple games just to get the feel of things. Ben had been busy getting adults to help out with various tasks for the home games. Frank and Jim, his two firemen friends, had willingly agreed to run the sideline markers. Roger was going to take care of chalking the boundary lines and yard lines, and last year's announcer agreed to take up his post again in the crow's nest, although he didn't seem very enthusiastic about doing it. Ben presumed, because of losing seasons over the past few years.

Chapter 18

The first game was a home game against Applewood. Applewood was a very small town, much smaller than Jordan, and notoriously not very good in football, although they had managed to beat Jordan rather handily last year. The boys practiced hard all week and seemed to be coming together as a team. The younger ones seemed to be picking things up quickly. Since they could only practice six on six, Ben knew that they were handicapped in not being able to practice against a full team, but that was the best he could do.

Thursday they had a light practice and then spent some time sorting through game uniforms, making sure everyone had pants and jerseys that would fit. There were plenty to pick from, but nothing was in great shape. Ben felt somewhat sorry for the boys, because this equipment didn't look very good. Their helmets were scuffed and chipped. The former coach had issued stars for good plays, which the players had displayed on their helmets. Ben previously had the boys remove the stickers, but dirty paste marks were still visible. Ben tried to remind himself that it is not the outside that counts, but what is on the inside[10].

On Friday morning to Ben's amazement, Mr. Reed announced the football game over the intercom in his morning announcements. It was merely a factual statement with no enthusiasm whatsoever. Ben was glad he was in his room with his science class, because he was certain there were many snide comments by students in the other classes. Ben had to remind himself of Rule 7 – "I will endure insults." He hoped his players would also remember this Rule in whatever classes they were attending.

---

[10] I Sam. 16:7 – ... "The Lord does not look at the things people look at. People look at the outward appearance, but the Lord looks at the heart." (NIV)

Late in the afternoon Ben went to the office and checked the boys' grades. He could feel his pulse rising as he pulled the list from his mail box. He slowly scanned the list and gave a sigh of relief when he reached the bottom and found that everyone had qualified. "Praise God," he said to himself.

Ben had requested that the boys meet in the locker room at 6:00 p.m. so that they would be ready in plenty of time for the 7:00 p.m. game. They went out and did their warm up exercises until about 6:40. Ben then had them exit the field and meet in the Bus Garage conference room. Ben had butterflies worse than he could ever remember. Even worse than at his wedding!

Applewood had a team of about 25 players. During warm-ups, Ben could tell they were probably a little bigger than Jordan, but not much. That was good, Ben rationalized. But, then there was the crowd. Applewood must have had 200 to 300 people. The visitor's bleachers were nearly full. Jordan's bleachers for the home team were considerably larger, but there were maybe 25 people there, and most of them appeared to be doubters and hecklers rather than supporters. Ben knew they had their work cut out for themselves. Somehow Ben needed to encourage his players, since they had observed the same things that he had.

Ben began his pre-game pep talk. "I'm going to start tonight just like we start every practice. We are going to review the rules, the rules that will help us bring honor to God.

Rule #1 – I will be a man of integrity

Rule #2 – I will encourage others

Rule #3 – I will bear other's burdens

Rule #4 – I will not speak unwholesome words

Rule #5 – I will work hard

Rule #6 – I will love my enemies

Rule #7 – I will endure insults

Rule #8 – I will not pollute my body

Rule #9 – I will be a team player

Rule #10 – I will enjoy life

"As I said before, these are the rules we play by, and these are the rules we live by. I expect you to abide by these rules when you play tonight. Remember, it is a privilege to play football for your school. You are representatives for your school and for God, so make a good impression before a watching world – or at least the portion of the world that is watching tonight! Any questions?"

Buck spoke up, "I think we are ready, Coach."

"Alright, let's go play football!"

The team re-entered the field and finished a few final warm up drills. The referees requested that the captains come forward for the coin toss. Ben had totally forgotten about that, so he quickly motioned for Buck and Tommy to be the captains, since they were the only seniors on the team. They met at center field, and the coin toss favored Applewood, who elected to receive the kickoff.

The announcer then introduced the starting players for each team. As he went through the lineup, it was soon apparent that Applewood's team was entirely juniors and seniors. In traditional fashion, the announcer introduced the home team last. As he read Jordan's line up, Ben could feel his face get flush. His team had more freshmen and sophomores than upper classmen. He suddenly knew that experience would be a problem, but he also knew that Satan liked to cast doubts whenever he got a chance.

As they huddled right before the kick-off, Ben said, "You guys have practiced hard for tonight, now let's honor God by how you play. Remember on offense to stay low on your blocks. On defense be aware of where the ball is, but also feel where they are moving you and react accordingly."

As his team took the field to kick-off, Ben said a silent prayer, "I pray, Lord, that you would keep these boys safe and that they would honor you by their play tonight. May they learn the value of team play, and may they enjoy the game. They have worked hard and have overcome a lot of obstacles to get to this point. Whether they win or lose, please bless them."

The referee blew his whistle, and the game was underway. Ben had appointed Cody to be the kicker for the game, and to Ben's amazement the kick was actually pretty good. Jordan rushed down the field, but Ben could suddenly see a hole developing that wasn't good. Appleton's receiver had made a good fake and then jolted to the opposite side of the field. It was enough to catch Jordan off guard and allow Appleton to race for their first touchdown. This was not a good start for Jordan's first outing. The extra point was good and it was suddenly 7 to 0 with only a few seconds off the clock. Ben could see some finger pointing going on with his players. Not the team attitude he was expecting.

As the game progressed, Jordan settled down and played better football than the opening play, but Appleton had rambled to a 20 to 0 lead midway into the third quarter. Jordan had a break when Sam intercepted a pass on Appleton's 20 yard line. On the very next play Zeke handed the ball to Rob for an end run on the right side. Jimmy made a fantastic block on the line backer and Rob ran in for the score. That was impressive, Ben thought, until he saw Rob spike the football in the end zone and point to himself like he was some super hero. It was like Rob thought no one else on the team had made any contribution to the play.

The announcer's enthusiasm picked up dramatically as he praised Rob over the loud speaker. "What a tremendous run by #22, Rob Blair! A 20 yard run and Jordan's first touchdown."

Throughout the game the announcer kept spewing out statistics on each of Jordan's players progress; number of yards gained, number of tackles, number of pass receptions. Ben realized that this was not at all conducive to promoting team play. It took every player to make a winning team, not just a few with big statistics.

About midway through the 4th quarter, Corky was running the ball up the middle. The center for Applewood made the tackle, but injured his ankle on the play. Corky spoke some inappropriate words and made a gesture as if to say "You got what you deserved." A couple of Applewood's players helped their teammate off the field, and then play resumed. Ben was appalled that after all their discussions about the rules, that his team would act opposite of what he was trying to teach them. The game finally ended 34 to 7, another loss for Jordan. Ben was frustrated to say the least, but he knew when he agreed to be the coach that he was biting off a big challenge.

In the locker room after the game everyone was playing the blame game. Ben realized he had a lot of work to do to make these boys into a team. Before the game he thought they were all working together well and helping each other out. But watching the game revealed a different story. Most of the boys were out for personal glory. Ben didn't say much to his team, except "That wasn't what I expected from you guys tonight. It doesn't matter so much to me that we lost the game as it does that we didn't play by the rules. We didn't accomplish our mission of bringing glory to the One who deserves it. I'll see all of you at practice on Monday." No one spoke after that. Everyone finished dressing and left for home.

Chapter 19

After a restless night, Ben finally got up and started making coffee. It was a sunny morning and as Ben was looking out his kitchen window at the birds searching for insects in the grass, he saw Ruth pull into his driveway. Ruth greeted him at the door with a plate of warm cinnamon rolls, another one of his favorites. He invited her in and they shared the rolls and coffee together. In the course of conversation she politely inquired, "How did the football game go last night?"

Ben suspected that she had already heard, but he replied honestly, "Well, we got beat pretty badly, which I guess is typical for Jordan. I'm not as concerned about the loss, though, as much as I am the boys' attitudes. It was not good, Ruth. I have tried to emphasize the rules every day and how important they are for football as well as for life, but last night proved that the rules weren't important to the boys. They were in it for their own personal glory."

Ruth replied after a thoughtful pause. "A war is seldom won by a single battle. The victory comes in perseverance."

Ben said, "I appreciate your advice. You always seem to have a lot of wisdom! Somehow I need something that will change their hearts. I know that only God can change hearts, but I feel responsible for these young men."

Ruth replied, "Do you remember Bobby Dyton, that little boy that we prayed for in church last Sunday?"

"Is he the 7 year old boy with leukemia?"

"Yes, I understand he is in very serious condition now. The doctors have done everything they can, but his only hope is for a bone marrow transplant. Since he is adopted, his parents are not a match and there are no known siblings, which would be the most likely candidates for him. Unless a matching donor is found soon, he isn't expected to live more than a few weeks. I've heard that Bobby loves football and his dream is to play on a high school football team someday. Maybe it would be an encouragement to Bobby if the football team paid him a visit in the hospital. It might also help your team to realize that they have the opportunity to do what some kids can only dream about doing. Hopefully, too, they might see the benefit of encouraging others. Rule #2 – right?"

"Ruth, I like your idea. Real life examples are always helpful, as I have discussed in my science class. I'll try and contact Bobby's parents today and see if they would be open to a team visit."

That afternoon Ben called the hospital. He introduced himself to Mike and Becky Dyton. "Hi, I'm Ben Harper, a teacher at Jordan High School. I'm also the new football coach. I'm so very sorry to hear about your son. I can't imagine the weight of your burden."

"Thank you, Mr. Harper, for your concern. Our little boy is very ill and we are desperately hoping that a bone marrow donor can be found soon."

Ben could tell from the tone of their voices that their hearts were very heavy. He hoped his request would not be rejected because of the desperate situation. "I understand that Bobby loves football."

"He loves football a lot. He used to carry a little football with him wherever he went. It was his favorite toy. He has always talked about playing football someday."

Then Ben could hear sobbing noises muffled, clearly expressions of heartache as they were realizing their son's dream would never come true. As if nudged by the Holy Spirit, Ben hesitantly asked, "Would you mind if I brought the football team to the hospital tomorrow afternoon to visit Bobby for a few minutes? Maybe it will give him a little encouragement."

"Oh, that would be great! We know he would love seeing them. "

"Great, we will plan to be there around 4:30."

On his way home from church on Sunday, Ben stopped at Walmart and bought a full sized football. He thought that maybe the team could present it to Bobby with all of their signatures. He hoped Bobby would enjoy it, although he had no idea what to expect.

On Monday all of the boys showed up in the locker room after school for practice as they typically did. As they entered, Ben was waiting for them. "There is no football practice tonight. Instead we are taking a field trip."

Buck questioned Ben's motive. "Coach, we lost big time on Friday night and you're saying we aren't going to practice. What's up with this?"

"I didn't say we aren't going to practice. We're going to practice something other than football tonight. We are going to practice Rule #2, which I did not see evident at all in our first game."

The boys looked bewildered. "Rule #2? You mean 'encourage others'?"

"Yes," Ben said, "I'm glad someone finally remembered. We are going to Central Hospital on the west side of Jordan. If I can get two or three guys to drive along with myself, I would appreciate it. We'll meet in the hospital lobby in 15 minutes."

The boys had no idea what Ben had planned. They brainstormed all kinds of ideas on the way to the hospital, but they all knew they could not anticipate what Coach was going to do. He was not like any other coach or teacher they had ever had before.

They all gathered in the lobby of the hospital exactly on time. Ben was carrying a sack with something good sized in it, but no one knew what it was. Ben explained, "We are going to pay a visit to Bobby Dyton. He is a 7 year old boy who has leukemia. He is in desperate need of a bone marrow transplant, but finding a matching donor in a short time is highly unlikely. He has probably coped with more difficulties in the first 7 years of his life than any of us has in our lives to date. His passion is football, so I thought what better way to make his day than to meet a real football team."

As the senior member of the team, Buck announced his resistance. "Coach, what are we supposed to say to him? We don't even know him. This is really awkward." The other boys nodded their heads in agreement.

Ben said, "I've not met Bobby before either, but that doesn't mean we can't show our concern and try to lift his spirits. If you don't know what to say, try asking a question. That is usually a good way to get things started. Just be yourselves – be real."

To the boys that sounded easier said than done. They reluctantly followed Ben up two flights of stairs to Room 203. They entered cautiously, not knowing what they would find. Bobby's parents were sitting next to Bobby's bed and Bobby was elevated to a half sitting position. There was a rack holding several bags of fluid next to his bed with numerous tubes extending to somewhere under the sheets. A machine was located next to his bed monitoring what appeared to be several different things. It made an annoying beep every once in a while.

Bobby was very frail looking. He probably didn't weigh more than 80 pounds, although his frame looked like he should be much bigger than that. All of his hair was gone and his eyes were sunken and dark. The boys recognized that these were all signs of someone that was very ill, deathly ill. But what they didn't expect was the huge smile on Bobby's face. He was beaming as the boys slowly migrated around Bobby's bed. For the moment he forgot about all the pain that wreaked havoc in his body and the dire circumstances that were facing him. He was overcome with joy!

Ben introduced himself as the high school football coach and then he had each of the boys introduce themselves and tell Bobby their grade in school and what position they played. Bobby was glued to each of the players with enthusiasm as they spoke. When the boys finished their introductions, Bobby blurted out, "And I'm Bobby Dyton, and someday I'm going to be a football player just like you!"

After seeing Bobby, they all knew the odds of that were like winning the mega lottery. Bobby started asking the boys about different plays and how the first game went. They were surprised at how much he knew about football, and even that he knew they had played their first game. The boys began interacting with Bobby. Ben could tell they were starting to feel more comfortable being around him. Their initial fears were beginning to evaporate. As the boys were talking to Bobby, Ben had an opportunity to talk to Mike and Becky.

"We so appreciate you and the team coming to visit Bobby. We didn't know if we should, but we told him this morning that you were coming after school. Since then, that is all he has been talking about. He was afraid he would fall asleep and miss them."

Ben said, "Thank you for allowing us to come. I can tell that Bobby has been an encouragement to the team. I'm amazed at his good attitude."

"He fully understands what will probably happen to him, and he has accepted this as God's plan, but he still remains positive about his situation."

"He is a remarkable child," Ben responded.

After 15 to 20 minutes of conversation Ben announced, "Bobby, it is about time for us to leave. We don't want to make you too tired. But before we go, we brought you a gift."

"What is it?" Bobby asked anxiously.

Ben pulled out a real football from the sack he had carried into the room. "Wow!" Bobby exclaimed. "Is that for me?"

"Yes, it sure is. And I'm going to have every player sign his name with a marker so you can remember all of them."

"This is great! I can't believe it. You guys actually got me a real football! You guys are awesome!"

Knowing that their performance was far from the greatest last Friday night, they were humbled by the thought that this little boy was thinking of them as being greater than they deserved. Before they left the room, Ben asked, "Would it be OK if I prayed for Bobby?"

His parents nodded in agreement. Almost instinctively they all held hands including Bobby as they formed a circle around his bed. When Ben concluded, they all individually shook Bobby's hand before they left.

Ben suggested that the boys re-convene in the lobby before they left the hospital. There wasn't a dry eye in the group. They all were overcome with emotions that they hadn't experienced in a long time. Buck finally broke the silence and said, "It isn't fair that Bobby has to suffer like that. He is only 7 years old. What has he ever done to deserve this?"

Ben hesitated for a moment and then replied. "Life isn't fair. God never promised that it would be. If life were fair, we would all be suffering greatly because of the sins we've committed. God has a purpose for every problem[11]. Some problems He uses to strengthen our character, some He uses to impact other people, and some He uses for reasons we don't even know. But through it all, we have to trust that God knows what He is dong and that in the end it is fulfilling His plan. God is sovereign. He is in control of all things."

---

[11] Rom. 8:28 – And we know that in all things God works for the good of those who love him, who have been called according to his purpose. (NIV)

"I just wish there was something we could do to help him," Corky said.

Zeke jumped in, "Coach, why don't all of us get tested to see if we are a bone marrow match for Bobby?" The other boys all agreed that getting tested was a good idea.

Ben replied, "It is a long shot, but it is certainly something we can try. Let's check with the nurse and see what we would have to do."

Ben approached the nurses' station. Mrs. Green, the head nurse, happened to be at the desk. Ben inquired, "We are all from Jordan High School. I'm the football coach and these boys are all members of the football team. We've just visited Bobby Dyton, and we understand he is in desperate need of a bone marrow transplant. We were wondering if we could all be tested to see if we might be a match for Bobby."

"Are any of you directly related to Bobby?"

"No," Ben replied with a pleading tone in his voice, "but if there is even a small chance that a non-relative could be a match, we'd like to be tested."

"Well, this is a noble thing you wish to do. We can certainly have all of you tested. We will need to take a swab inside your mouth so we can determine if your DNA is a close match to Bobby's DNA. If you would like, we can do it right now. It will only take a few minutes."

Ben turned to the boys, and they were more than willing to proceed with taking the DNA samples. Ben replied to Mrs. Green, "Yes, we'd all like to do that."

Mrs. Green took a sample from Ben first and then from each of the boys. "We appreciate you doing this, but please don't be disappointed. Unless you are a close relative, it would take a miracle for any of you to be a match. The parameters we have to match for Bobby are very rare. Because time is critical for Bobby, we will rush the analysis. Hopefully we should have the results tomorrow. We'll let you know as soon as we find out."

"Thanks, Mrs. Green," Ben said. "We'll be waiting on your call."

They all quietly left the hospital that evening. Though sadness was on their hearts, Ben marveled that twelve players had reluctantly entered a young boy's room to encourage him. They had left his room as one team inspired by a young boy they had suddenly come to love. God does work in mysterious ways!

Chapter 20

About noon on Tuesday, Ben received a call from Mrs. Green at the hospital. "Mr. Harper, I can't believe this but Buck is a match for Bobby! This is truly a miracle – the timing and a near perfect match – it's just incredible!"

"Wow that is fantastic!" Ben exclaimed.

Mrs. Green continued, "If Buck is still willing to donate, we will need consent from his parents, since he is under 18 years old. We would like him to come to the hospital tomorrow for some additional testing and prep work. Then we will draw the bone marrow on Thursday morning and perform the transplant. Buck can return to school on Friday, but he will need to take it easy for a couple days. Within a week or so he should be back to normal."

"Mrs. Green that is wonderful news. I have Buck in my science class after lunch. I will talk to him then. We'll get back to you very soon."

"Thanks, Mr. Harper. You and your team have been a real inspiration for Bobby."

Ben could hardly wait for science class so he could talk to Buck. Class went well, but Ben was having trouble focusing. As class adjourned, Ben gave the next assignment and then said, "Buck, would you stay after class for a few minutes? I need to talk to you." The other students didn't think anything about it, assuming it was football related.

"Buck, I had a call from Mrs. Green at the hospital a couple hours ago. Buck, she said you are a match for Bobby!"

For a moment Buck was speechless. Then he mustered the words, "Really? I figured we were just going through the motions for nothing. This is great, Mr. Harper. What do I have to do?"

"First, you have to get consent from your parents, since you are under 18. Do they know that you were tested?"

Buck suddenly had a stricken look on his face. "Coach, I only have a Mom. My dad left when I was only 2 years old. I've never seen him after that, and I don't even remember what he looked like. My Mom has taken care of me ever since. Because she works a lot, we don't communicate much. So, no, I haven't even mentioned it to her. I'll talk to her as soon as I get home. Will it be a problem that I don't have a dad to give consent?"

"Under the circumstances, I don't think that will be a problem, but I will check with the nurse for you."

Buck suddenly realized the impact of what just happened. "Coach, I have a chance to save Bobby's life! I really hope it works! Coach, can we tell the other guys at practice tonight? I'm sure they will all be anxious to hear the news."

"Yes, I'm sure they will want to know."

Buck said, "I have one request, though."

"What is that, Buck?"

"I would like my name to be kept secret, except among the guys. If it is somehow announced to the public, can we just say it was a team effort?"

"That is very humble of you, Buck. I like the sound of 'team'! That will be our story."

At practice that afternoon, Ben called all the guys together. "Before we go out, I have an announcement that I would like to make. Mrs. Green from the hospital called me today and ---- we have a match for Bobby! They have determined that Buck is a very close match to Bobby's bone marrow. They have to do some more tests tomorrow, but if all of that checks out OK, they will do the procedure Thursday morning."

The boys were elated as they heard the news. "Way to go Buck! You're our man!" Zeke said. "Does that mean Bobby will live?"

Ben replied, "Well, there are no guarantees, but this certainly gives him a much better chance. There are always risks, but normally bone marrow transplants are successful."

Buck asked for a moment to speak. "Two years ago, one year ago, not even six months ago would I have even considered going into Bobby's room. My heart would have said, 'That's not my problem. I don't even know him, so why should I care'. But some things have been happening lately that are hard to explain. Coach's rules are teaching us to care for and help others. I've never had that attitude before, until now. I think Bobby touched all of our lives, and now we have a chance to touch his. I want to ask every one of you to not tell anyone that it is me donating bone marrow for Bobby. We are doing this as a team. So if anyone asks, let's just say that it was a team effort. I'm not a hero, and you are not a hero. We are all the same. We're just people that want to help Bobby. Is everyone in agreement with this?"

Everyone responded heartily to Buck's comments and agreed not to tell anyone. Ben said to the group, "Buck will have to miss a few practices after the procedure, but he should be back to full strength in a week or so. Since there is no game this week due to the break between trimesters, this should work out OK."

When Buck went home that night, he immediately found his mom. "Mom, can I talk to you for a few minutes?"

Chapter 21

Buck's mom worked at the local grocery store trying to make ends meet. In the evenings she had to catch up on all the house work. "I really have to get this laundry done tonight, Buck. Can we do it some other time?"

"Mom, this is really important. Can I help you with the laundry and maybe we can talk while we work?"

Buck never helped with household chores, so his mom was shocked when he offered to help. "You must have something pretty important if you're willing to help with laundry!"

"I do, Mom. I really need to talk to you." And so Buck began with his story. "We have this new science teacher, Mr. Harper, at school this year. At first I didn't like him, but he is a really great guy. We pleaded with him, and he finally agreed to be our football coach. Before the season started he told us we had to live by a higher standard to honor God. He gave us this list of 10 rules that we are supposed to follow. The rules include encouraging others, bearing others' burdens, being a team player, and some others. He said they would help us to live our lives better, not just be better players. When we played last Friday night, some of us weren't even thinking about the rules. We didn't play as a team. We disregarded almost everything he told us. The game was a total disaster. After the game, he didn't get mad like all of our other coaches. He's different. He really seems to care about us. Anyway, Monday after school instead of making us practice extra hard, he took all of us to the hospital to visit a 7 year old boy, Bobby Dyton."

"Isn't that the little boy with leukemia?" his mom asked.

"Yeah, it is. Do you know him?"

"No, but I've heard others talk about him at the grocery store. It sounds like he has been very sick."

"None of us were thrilled about going to see some 7 year old that we didn't even know. I think Coach wanted us to see that we need to think about other people more than ourselves. When we walked into Bobby's room, he had this great big smile on his face. He couldn't wait to see us. He thought we were the greatest. He was adopted by his mom and dad when he was only a baby. He is their only child. Coach told us that his only hope of surviving is to have a bone marrow transplant. The problem is his bone marrow is very hard to match and so far no donor has been found. After we left Bobby's room, we all decided that we wanted to be tested to see if any of us might be compatible. And so we did, all of us, even Coach. Coach received a call from the nurse today, and she told him that I'm a match! She said it would be a miracle if any of us would be a match, but it happened! But there is only one thing – since I'm under 18, I need your permission to do this. Please Mom, will you let me help Bobby? It may be his only chance to live. They said I'd be a little tired for a couple days, but then by a week or so I should be totally back to normal. Mom, I really want to do this."

Buck's mom had never seen him this excited about anything before. She saw the tear in his eye, and she could feel tears were forming in her own eyes. Reflections of an earlier day in her own life were flooding her soul. Sometime her story would have to be told, but not today. "Buck," she said, "I think that you are doing a very noble thing. I will certainly give you my permission. If you can help that little boy that would be one of the greatest things you could ever do."

"Mom, thank you so much. I promise to do much more around here to help you. I'm sorry that I haven't done better until now."

Buck's mom could see a huge change in Buck's attitude, just his willingness to talk was very abnormal. She remembered years ago when Buck entered her life. She couldn't imagine life without him now. She also couldn't imagine this other family without their son either. She said, "I'm proud of you, Buck, for wanting to help this little boy."

Buck went to the hospital the next morning and went through the additional testing and informational meetings with various hospital staff members. During the process Mrs. Green, the head nurse, asked him, "Buck, do you want us to release your name as being the bone marrow donor for Bobby? That is up to you. Some people are OK with releasing their name and others prefer to keep it confidential. Either way, we will honor your request."

Buck replied, "If anything is released, please just say it was the high school football team. I don't want my name released. We are a real team now and I would like to keep it that way."

"Very well, Buck, the team it shall be!"

Buck was instructed to be at the hospital by 6:30 a.m. the following morning, and that the actual procedure would be performed around 8:00 a.m. Buck's mom took off work so she could be with him during the procedure. Buck was glad for that. He'd never been in a hospital that he could remember, and it all felt a bit foreign to him. The procedure went as scheduled with no complications. Buck didn't wake up from the anesthesia until about noon. Once he was fairly coherent, the nurse reported to him, "Your bone marrow has already been transplanted into Bobby, and so far he is doing well. It will take a day or so before we can really tell if it is going to work."

Buck said, "How soon before I can see him?"

"If you are feeling well after school tomorrow, why don't you stop by then?"

"Sounds great, Mrs. Green. Thanks," Buck replied, still in a bit of a daze.

Buck went to school the next day and to practice after school, but he didn't participate. He needed to rest a couple days before getting back into the routine. At practice Ben had a few announcements to make to the team. "First, I'd like to report that Buck successfully donated his bone marrow for Bobby, and the transplant went very well. It will be a day or two before they can tell if Bobby is going to be OK. And to Buck, I just want to say that was a true act of kindness and love."

They all chimed in with "Way to go, Buck!"

Buck replied, "It was a team effort. I wouldn't have even gone to the hospital if it hadn't been for Coach. And I wouldn't have been tested, if it hadn't been for all of you. So, it is truly a team effort."

Chapter 22

Ben told the boys, "Before we practice tonight I want to teach you a new word. It is an Indian word '*ieb-sw-lepte*'."

Jokingly Will said, "What tribe is that from?"

"I'm glad you asked, Will. It is from the tribe of Jordan."

"But," Will said, "we are the Jordan Indians."

"That's right, and this is our word. We should be free to make up any word we want, right? Isn't that how languages began?"

"What does it mean?" Corky asked.

"I've broken it down into three parts so it will be easier to remember. *ieb-sw-lepte* stands for our 10 rules. It will help you to remember them." On the board Ben wrote:

1 i = man of integrity
2 e = encourage others
3 b = bear others' burdens
4 s = not speak unwholesome words
5 w = work hard
6 l = love my enemies
7 e = endure insults
8 p = not pollute my body
9 t = team player
10 e = enjoy life

"I want each of you to know the rules forwards and backwards. Our goal is to live by a higher standard in order to honor God. We can't effectively do that unless we live by the rules. I want you to know them by number also. So, for example, if I say #5, you should automatically know that means 'I will work hard'. You'll find out later, but this is very important. Any questions about that? We'll review these from time to time, so be prepared."

After practice Buck and a few of the guys went to see Bobby at the hospital. They thought it would not be good to have the whole team go, since he might not be totally recovered from his procedure yet. "Hi guys!" Bobby said with great enthusiasm as he saw them enter his room.

Buck quickly asked, "How are you doing, Bobby?"

"Oh, I'm beginning to feel a lot better. The doctor said it could take a couple of days to notice any change, but I can already tell it is working."

"That's great," Buck said. All the guys had a good time talking to Bobby. He was probably more of an encouragement to them than they were to him. A real bond was developing between Bobby and the team.

Suddenly Bobby said, "I heard that someone on the football team donated their bone marrow for me. Is that true?"

The players all looked at each other remembering their pledge of secrecy. Finally Sam responded, "It was a team effort, Bobby. We all played a part."

"Mom," Bobby said with a quizzical look on his face, "is that possible? Can a whole team donate bone marrow?"

"Well Bobby, I don't know how it all worked, but I know one thing, with God anything is possible!"

That seemed to satisfy Bobby's curiosity, at least for the moment. The group didn't stay too long, because they could tell Bobby was getting tired. Buck initiated their departure. "Bobby, we'll be back to visit you soon."

Bobby replied with a gleam in his eye, "Thanks, guys, I'll be rooting for you next Friday!" That meant a lot to the boys. At least they had one loyal fan.

Chapter 23

Over the weekend Ben had some errands to run. Without a game on Friday, he had a little more time to focus on some new ideas. He could tell that since the ordeal with Bobby, the guys were starting to come together as a team, but he felt compelled to take some additional measures to ensure that they didn't lose their team focus.

Ben drove to his first stop, the Jordan Chronicle. This was the local newspaper that covered various activities around town as well as all the local sports events. It contained all the league standings, the outcomes of all the games on Friday night, and a complete tabulation of each player's statistics (points scored, number of tackles, yards gained, etc.). Ben could sense from the first game that publishing individual statistics was going to be a detriment to the team. It was a temptation to try and rise above others on the team.

"Can I help you?" the receptionist asked as Ben entered the small office building in downtown Jordan. The receptionist's desk was very well organized, much in contrast to the rest of the offices that Ben could see. There were newspapers and note pads scattered in various places on the floor, and most waste baskets were overflowing. Ben could see several cubicles with numerous clippings pinned to the partitions separating the offices.

"Yes," Ben said, "I was wondering if I might talk to your sports editor."

"That is Mr. Baxter," she said. "I'll see if he is available."

Within a few minutes, a rather stocky man with dark hair approached Ben wearing blue jeans and a polo shirt that was at least one size too small. The shirt obviously enhanced his muscular physique, which Ben assumed was the intended purpose. "Hello sir, I'm George Baxter. How can I help you?"

Ben knew his request would be very unconventional, but he was determined to present his case. "Mr. Baxter, my name is Ben Harper from Jordan High. I'm the new football coach and I wanted ..."

Before he could continue, Mr. Baxter cut him off. With a bit of a chuckle he said, "So you are the one who volunteered to lead those renegades! Good luck in making anything out of those guys. You might have a couple decent players if they get their act together, but that won't do you much good in this conference this year. There are some big teams and some really good teams. I predict that Jordan won't even score against any of the conference teams. My reporter told me you scored once in the first non-conference game, but that must have been a mistake on someone's part. How many players do you have, Mr. Harper?"

"Well, Mr. Baxter, we have one team."

"Yeah, but how many players are on your one team?"

"I have twelve players, Mr. Baxter, and they are not renegades, they are boys with great value."

"Well, we'll see if you can still claim that statement at the end of the season. Whoever heard of a football team with only twelve players! That's absurd! My daughter's ballet class has more members than that."

"Mr. Baxter, I have a request to make. I know it is tradition to report all of the statistics for each of the players in the conference. I know that people look at that stuff, and they tend to make heroes out of players that aren't. I want to request that you not report individual statistics for my Jordan players."

"Why would I do that?" Mr. Baxter asked sarcastically. "Are you afraid there won't be any?"

"In the spirit of teamwork, it would be better for my players if you didn't report this information."

"Well, Mr. Harper, the answer to your request is 'No'! The people expect this kind of information to be reported, and we intend to give it to them."

Ben left the newspaper office a bit disappointed, but he wasn't totally surprised. That is why his next stop was important.

His next stop was at the Shirt Shop. The Shirt Shop printed all kinds of funny shirts with pictures and slogans. They did a lot of neat stuff, but Ben wasn't interested in that. The store owner, Mr. Stevens, approached him and inquired if he could help. The owner was a middle aged man, well groomed, and obviously in good physical shape. He was dressed like a successful businessman. Ben introduced himself, "I'm Ben Harper. I teach science classes at Jordan High, and I'm also the football coach – new coach, that is."

"Sounds like coaching could be a real challenge considering recent years. I thought they cancelled the program after last year?"

"Well, they did," Ben said, "but a group of boys really wanted to play. I presented our case to the school and they agreed to allow the program to continue with some stipulations. Anyway, I came to see if I might get twelve white and twelve red shirts that we could use for our team jerseys."

"I'm sure I can accommodate that. What numbers and names do you want printed on them?"

Ben said, "Oh that is the easy part. I don't want anything printed on them, just plain shirts."

"I've never heard of football jerseys without names and numbers," Mr. Stevens said.

"Well, I'm a science teacher and I like experiments. This will be an experiment, but on the football field rather than in the science class."

Mr. Stevens observed, "I sense that your experiment involves something more than football! Since you don't want anything printed on the shirts and since I'm aware that the school has a tight budget, I am more than willing to donate the shirts toward your cause. Just let me know how your experiment turns out!"

Ben was overwhelmed by his gracious gift. As he picked out the various sizes that he needed, Ben turned to Mr. Stevens and said, "Thank you so much. I really appreciate this. This is a real blessing. If you want to see the outcome of the experiment, please come to our football games on Friday nights."

"I might just do that!"

Chapter 24

Football practice the following week was really good. All of the boys were working hard and really playing together, something that they hadn't done the first game. Buck was getting stronger and it appeared would be at full strength by Friday. The team was definitely at a disadvantage, though, with only twelve members. The hardest part of practice was that they couldn't run plays against a full team. They improvised the best they could, but it still wasn't like a real scrimmage. Ben used traffic cones to simulate the missing players. That helped to visualize positions, but traffic cones didn't offer any resistance. It wasn't like the real thing, but it would have to do.

Their next opponent was Gridley. Gridley was also a non-conference opponent, but they were historically known for their trash talk on the field, according to Frank and Jim, Ben's firemen friends. Ben was a bit nervous that this might lead to some confrontations during the game. The boys were really coming around, and he didn't want them to be provoked by the evil words of an opponent. Therefore, all week he stressed Rule #7 – "I will endure insults." Gridley was also an away game, which would normally be seen as a disadvantage. But since Ben didn't expect many Jordan fans to attend, it probably wouldn't make that much difference.

Throughout the week, the boys made a special effort to stay in touch with Bobby. He was doing well, getting stronger every day. Everyone was thrilled with his progress.

Ben and the team left Jordan with plenty of time to spare on Friday. Gridley was only about 30 minutes away, but by the time they packed all the equipment in their vehicles and made the journey, the time seemed to go by quickly. They had to car pool with their own vehicles, since there was no budget for a bus.

When they arrived at Gridley High School, they were directed to the locker room by the janitor. He was a fairly friendly man, although he looked a bit astonished at the caravan of vehicles and the small number of boys. As the boys began getting dressed, Ben made a surprise announcement. "Could I have your attention? We have new jerseys for the team courtesy of the 'Shirt Shop' in Jordan! So, from now on, we will be wearing these for our games rather than our old ones from previous years."

"Wow, Coach, how did you do that?" they all asked.

"Well, I just told the store owner our situation and he volunteered to donate them."

Russ said a bit nervously, "They forgot to put our numbers on them. They are just plain shirts!"

"I'm glad you noticed, Russ," Ben said. "This is going to be our new look. If we are truly going to be a team, then it doesn't matter who scores the points or who makes the most tackles. Whatever we do, it is going to be a team effort. Without numbers, it won't be as easy for us or anyone else to keep track of individual statistics. If we win, we win as a team, and if we lose we lose as a team. Remember Rule #9?"

"Rule 9. I will be a team player," Zeke said.

"Good," Ben replied, "you remembered."

"I think this is a good idea!" Rob exclaimed. "It is like we are one player rather than twelve."

"That's right, Rob. And I want you to play as one tonight and every night. Let's go out and get warmed up. At twenty minutes before game time, we'll come back to the locker room to go over a few things."

As they ran onto the field the crowd, which nearly filled the bleachers, began booing and yelling all kinds of derogatory comments. "Why did you guys even show up? Is this the grade school team? You can't even afford numbers on your jerseys?

Come on, we want a real team!" Then there was roaring laughter. Ben expected some of this from the opposing players, but certainly not from the fans. Ben realized this game was going to be as much mental as physical. The boys managed to get through warm-ups and then headed back to the locker room.

After their experience on the field, Ben wasn't sure where to start with his pre-game comments to the boys, but he mustered some courage and began. "I brought a little device with me tonight." Ben reached into his pocket and pulled out a small item, and held it up for the boys to see. "Who knows what this is?"

Tommy said, "It looks like a valve stem from a tire!"

"You are exactly right, Tommy. What is the function of a valve stem?"

Will volunteered, "It holds the air in a tire."

"That's right, but what does it do on a bigger scale?"

They all looked puzzled, so Ben explained. "A valve stem is certainly responsible for keeping air in a tire, but it is also responsible for keeping the car so it will move freely. A car with a flat tire cannot accomplish much, but a car with inflated tires can accomplish a lot. It can perform the way it was designed to perform. Each car has four valve stems. If one of them doesn't work, the whole car suffers, because it can't do what it was made to do. A valve stem is a very tiny part compared to all the parts that make up a car. But without it, the car is helpless. A valve stem doesn't get much glory, not like the engine, or the fancy interior, or the pretty paint job. A valve stem quietly does its job without seeking any accolades. I view each of you like this valve stem. Except instead of four, we have twelve. As long as each one of you does your job as part of the team, we will function well. But if you lose focus, then the team will be flat and won't accomplish what we are capable of doing. Since our last game, you guys have changed a lot. I believe you have truly become a team. You've already gotten a taste of what the other team plans to do. They are going to hassle you all night with derogatory comments. They are going to try and make you lose your focus. They are going to try and make you go flat. I believe if you play by our rules, they will leave this game embarrassed. Tonight you are going to have plenty of opportunities to show love to your enemy (Rule #6), endure insults (Rule #7), and hopefully to enjoy the game (Rule #10). If you let their comments get to you, and you respond in anger and frustration, then we've lost our mission – to bring glory to God. I challenge you to play by our rules tonight and see what happens. Remember the valve stem; it doesn't take a big thing to do a big thing! Any questions?"

No one made a sound. Ben could tell they were already battling emotions and temptations from the pre-game warm up. Ben knew in a few minutes he would find out how each player decided to respond. He prayed silently that God would empower them to play by the rules.

"One final thing," Ben said, "when the referee asks for the captains to come to center field for the coin toss, I want all of you to go. We are one team, no one is above another."

They all returned to the field to finish their warm up drills. When the referee asked for the captains, they all responded as Ben had instructed them. Gridley had three seniors as their captains, so when Ben's entire team met them they were a bit intimated. The referee had a weird look on his face, but he didn't say anything. Gridley won the toss and elected to receive.

Suddenly one of the referees approached Ben on the sidelines. "Your boys must have numbers on their jerseys. You can't field a team without numbered jerseys."

Ben replied, "There is nothing in the Rule Book that says we have to have numbers. Here, I have the Rule Book if you want to check."

Taken back a bit by Ben's knowledge of the rules, he said, "And what am I supposed to do if one of your players commits a penalty? I won't have a number to call out."

"That's not a problem," Ben said, "just call it on the team." Frustrated, the referee went back onto the field.

Ben huddled his team together before the kick-off. "Talk to each other out there. Help each other out. If you are having trouble, let me know and we will adjust somehow. We're a team. Let's play like a team. Remember that being able to play football is a privilege, a privilege that many kids don't have, like Bobby. Let's play for all of them tonight. Alright, let's go!"

Everyone took their positions, and the referee blew his whistle to start the game. Ben's stomach was fluttering nearly as bad as the first game. He prayed that tonight might be a game changer for the boys, but in his heart he knew the game was going to be a real challenge.

Cody kicked off. It was not a real long kick, but it was high, which gave Jordan a little extra time to get down field. A Gridley player caught the ball and took off straight up the middle. Jordan funneled quickly to the middle and made a great gang tackle. The opponent was starting on the 35 yard line. Ben could tell immediately that the Gridley team was well organized and well disciplined. They had a perfect circle for a huddle. They broke huddle and approached the line like a marching band. They all went down in formation in perfect unison.

Gridley's verbal attack on the field was ceaseless. Ben could hear many of the comments, and they were brutal. The jeers from the crowd were nearly as bad. Ben couldn't ever remember seeing or hearing about a game where the ridicule was so severe. Ben, however, was proud of his players. For the most part they were tuning out all of the negative chatter and were really focusing on playing good hard football. Several times they had offered a helping hand to the Gridley players after being tackled. Usually they refused the help, but a couple times the players had accepted.

It was almost the end of the first half. Neither team had taken many chances. There was still no score in the game, but

Gridley had the ball on Jordan's twenty yard line with one minute to play. They kept running the ball where Jordan had their smallest players. The boys were working well together, but the first half was beginning to take its toll physically on them. With only one substitute, it was impossible to give anyone much of a rest.

On fourth down with only 10 seconds remaining in the half, the Gridley fullback pounded his way through the right side of the line and scored. By the roar of the crowd and jubilation of the Gridley players you would have thought they had just won the Super Bowl. The fullback ran back and forth in the end zone making insinuations like he was the greatest. He also got right in the face of several Jordan players yelling, "What a bunch of wimps! You guys don't deserve to be here. Go home!"

The extra point kick was good and the half ended. Ben took his team to the locker room where they could talk and rest. As everyone took a seat, Ben could tell they were exhausted, and rightly so. "You guys have played a great game so far. Except for that last run, you've contained them on every play. Remember our mission is to honor God. You are doing a great job in not yielding to their standard of conduct. I'm sure everyone can see that you are living by a higher standard. Keep up the good work! All of their trash talk and ridicule is merely wasted energy."

Corky spoke up, "Coach, they are like a machine out there! They are really hard to stop."

"I know, Corky, but a machine is always predictable, at least one that is running properly, which I'm sure they think they are. Perhaps we can use this to our advantage. I've noticed that they are playing man to man defense on our receivers and their linebackers are keying on our running backs. So, let's juggle things up a bit and see what happens. From the very beginning of the season we've said we have to be flexible with only twelve players. All of you can play multiple positions. If we switch our receivers with our guards, for example, I suspect they won't know what to do. Likewise, we can also switch our running backs with our linemen.

Let's keep them guessing the second half. Remember to feel the play, just like we practiced with the blind folds. Feel where they are trying to move you and react accordingly. Keep talking to each other and back each other up. You are doing fine. Keep hanging in there."

They re-entered the field to the same verbal harassment as when the game started. Ben felt sorry for the boys, since only a handful of fans had come from Jordan. On the other hand, maybe it was a good thing, or there may have been a huge fight break out. That wasn't at all what Ben was trying to promote. A few more cheering fans would have been nice, though.

Just before the second half began, the referee that had approached Ben about having no numbers on the jerseys was walking along the sideline near Ben. Ben approached him and in a polite voice said, "Well, how is it working out with no numbers?"

He replied, "Actually, I like it. It makes things a lot easier for us. I think every school should do it!"

"That probably won't happen," Ben said. And then the whistle blew to start the second half. Ben hoped his team had the energy it was going to take to finish the game. Gridley seemed relentless with their substitutions. It was doubtful that any one player played more than half a game. Their players were always fresh.

Ben's idea of mixing up players had certainly caught the Gridley defense by surprise. They often looked confused, not knowing who they were supposed to watch. Their well oiled machine was not running as smoothly as normal. Late in the third quarter, Zeke was quarterback on a third down play. Rob, who normally played halfback, had moved to the right end. Zeke rolled right, first faking what appeared to be a deep pass, and then kept the ball for a run around the right side. Rob made a good block on the defensive end, but then turned around and received a quick handoff from Zeke. It was a reverse play that caught Gridley totally off guard. Rob was now running around the left end, while the Gridley team was still trying to figure out who had the ball. In the open Rob was faster than any player on the field. Because Gridley assumed it was a run to the right, they were now all on the wrong side of the field. Rob sprinted 40 yards for an easy touchdown. The Gridley coach was furious. He was yelling and spewing all kinds of profanities at his players. Oblivious to all that, the entire Jordan team was celebrating together in the end zone – no personal glory, but a true team celebration.

Since Jordan wasn't good at kicking extra points, they opted to run the ball. If successful, they would get the two point conversion, giving them a one point lead. But Jordan's attempt failed and the score was 7 to 6 in favor of Gridley.

After Jordan scored, Ben noticed that the Gridley players weren't as vocal with their trash talk as they were earlier. They were beginning to realize that Jordan came to play football and that verbal abuse wasn't going to alter their mission.

Midway through the fourth quarter Ben also detected some dissention among the Gridley players. They were starting to blame each other for unsuccessful plays. Jordan had not been the push-over opponent they had expected.

On a third down play Gridley ran their fullback up the center. They only needed a two yard gain for a first down. Almost every time on short yardage they had run the same play – like a machine, they were predictable. Ben motioned his team to be prepared for the run. Sure enough, Gridley ran as expected. But, Buck and Tommy were ready. They tackled the fullback for a two yard loss. The Gridley team was definitely frustrated. Their fullback was almost never stopped for a loss. They were kicking the turf and arguing with one another as they went back to the huddle. In their frustration they all failed to notice that their fullback was still on the ground. He had twisted his ankle and was having a very difficult time getting up. Buck looked at Tommy and they spontaneously went over and helped the injured fullback to his feet. He was unable to walk, so Buck and Tommy got on each side of him, like crutches, and helped him over to his team's bench. When they got to the sidelines, Buck said, "I'm sorry about your ankle. I really hope you are OK. You played a good game tonight."

The fullback was dumbfounded. He did not know how to respond. He had been tormenting the Jordan players all night with his obnoxious comments. They had never attempted any kind of retaliation, and now they were helping him! All he could muster was "Thank you."

Jordan got the ball one final time as the fourth quarter was drawing to a close, but they were unable to score. The game ended Gridley 7, Jordan 6. Jordan took the initiative to shake the hand of every Gridley player before they left the field. The Gridley players were amazingly quiet for just having won their second game. Even their coach was without words as Ben crossed the field and congratulated him on their victory. Jordan also made a special effort to thank each of the referees for doing a good job officiating the game.

As Ben's team left the field for the locker room, he could tell they had played with all the energy they had. There wasn't a clean spot on anyone's uniform. They almost looked like coal miners leaving for home. They were dragging, and they were disappointed.

One of the referees ran to catch Ben before he left the field. "Coach, I just want to tell you that when you and your team came onto the field tonight, I thought it was a joke. You were totally outnumbered, you really didn't look like a team, and with all the derogatory comments from the fans and the team – well, I just thought this can't be much of a game. But, I apologize for my hasty judgment. Your guys played an outstanding game. They played their hearts out. I've never been thanked by a losing team for doing a good job. In fact I've never been thanked by a winning team! Your team showed a lot of courage and gained a lot of respect tonight. You've done a great job with these boys. You should be proud of them. I hope you have a great season!"

Ben was grateful that someone noticed they were different than other teams. Hopefully others would eventually see a difference also.

Back in the locker room there wasn't much conversation. Seeing the somber mood, Ben spoke up, "Great game, guys!"

Zeke responded, "But we lost again."

Ben paused as he observed his team. "You didn't lose; you just didn't score as many points as the other team. The game you guys played tonight was the best team effort I have ever seen – by any team in any sport! You have no reason at all to be ashamed. When you guys helped their fullback off the field when he injured his ankle - that was a crowning moment. Did you notice that the harassing comments from the Gridley players suddenly stopped? Even their fans became silent. Do you know why? I'll tell you, because no one has ever done that before. That is called loving your enemy – Rule #6. In the world's view 'loving your enemy' doesn't' have any meaning. They don't know what to do with it. With your conduct tonight you changed the attitude of an entire team. That is what I call victory. I'm proud of every one of you! Now let's remember Rule #10. Did you enjoy the game tonight?" They all shook their heads in agreement. Suddenly they didn't seem to feel so bad.

Chapter 25

At practice on Monday Ben just had a light workout, since he knew they were still recuperating physically. They spent some time helping each other with homework. They all had been doing well keeping their grades up, but Ben knew that persistence was required if they were all going to remain eligible. Ben sensed that the boys even enjoyed doing better in school.

When they finished, Buck announced that he was going to stop at the hospital to visit Bobby. He invited the others to join him. Several had to get home, but the others were eager to go. Ben was glad to see that they had taken a liking to Bobby. It was good for all of them. He made a mental note that he, too, needed to check in with Bobby and his parents.

Jordan's next opponent was the town of Franklin. This would be Jordan's first conference game, and it was going to be a home game. Ben was glad for that. Coordinating vehicles and drivers for out of town games took time and energy that Ben would rather use in preparing for the game. Ben didn't know much about Franklin except they always seemed to have an above average record. They were a solid football team, nothing fancy, but they always seemed to get the job done.

Ben noticed a little more excitement at school after a near win at Gridley. The news that someone on the football team had donated bone marrow for Bobby Dyton also seemed to spur more interest in the football team. For his team's sake Ben hoped a few more fans would show up for the game.

On Thursday evening after practice Ben went to the hospital to visit Bobby. He hoped none of the players showed up while he was there, because he wanted to talk to Bobby's parents alone.

Ben entered Bobby's room, greeted with a huge smile and a hug from Bobby. Bobby said, "I heard you almost beat Gridley last Friday night. That is great! I knew you had a good football team."

It was hard not to love a kid who was always so positive. After fifteen minutes of game talk, Ben said, "Would it be OK with you if I talked to your mom and dad for a few minutes?"

"Sure, Mr. Harper, they need to talk to an adult once in a while."

Ben and Bobby's parents stepped out into the hallway while Bobby resumed his TV program. "How's Bobby doing?" Ben asked.

Mike said, "The doctors feel he is responding very well. He's had a lot more energy than before. They even said we can take him home in the morning. We just can't take him more than 20 – 30 minutes away from the hospital in case there is a sudden problem of some kind. He has to come back to the hospital frequently for checkups; more at first, then they taper off if everything continues to go well."

"That's great!" Ben said. "I wanted to see what you thought about bringing Bobby to the football game Friday night. The weather is supposed to be very nice and I thought he might enjoy something different."

Mike and Becky looked at each other with tears in their eyes. Almost in unison they replied, "That would be wonderful!" But Mike added, "He will have to be in a wheelchair."

"That is no problem," Ben said. "I would like him to be down on the sidelines with the team, if that is alright with you? You can be with him the whole time, and if he gets tired you can leave whenever you want."

"That sounds perfect," Mike said. "I think we'll wait until late Friday afternoon to tell him in case something happens in the mean time. We don't want to get his hopes up and then not be able to go."

Then Becky said, "Mr. Harper, thank you so much. You and the team have been such a blessing to Bobby and to us. Without your team's bone marrow, Bobby probably wouldn't be here."

"Well," Ben replied, "I appreciate all that you and Bobby have done for the team. After meeting Bobby, the players had a real change of heart. They are not the same boys they used to be. So, I thank you too."

On Friday afternoon Ben was feeling good, especially knowing or hoping that Bobby was going to attend. During Ben's afternoon study hall at 2:00 p.m., it was his custom to check the previous week's grades for each of his players. All of his players had been consistently doing "C" work or better, which had been a huge improvement for most of them. But today his heart sank when he saw that Wes, one of his freshmen, had received a "D" in math. There was a big test last week and apparently Wes had not done well. Now Ben found himself in a dilemma. He really needed Wes on the team. With only eleven players it was going to be really hard to even have a chance at winning, especially if one of the eleven got injured. On the other hand if he ignored his pre-season requirement that every player maintain a "C" average, then he would not be complying with his own rule that everyone needed to be a man of integrity. He had to show the team that the rules had to apply no matter how difficult the situation or no matter how great the temptation. He would have to tell Wes and the team before they got dressed for the game. This was not going to be easy for him or for the boys.

As the boys congregated in the locker room, Ben made the announcement with as firm a voice as he could muster. "I'm sad to inform you tonight that I have some negative news to report. I found out this afternoon that Wes didn't make a 'C' average in math last week. That means he won't be able to play tonight."

Wes had known about his grade, but he somehow hoped that Coach would overlook it and merely let him play. But he also knew that Coach was a man of his word, so his decision didn't come as a total surprise. Even though it hurt him dearly that he couldn't play, he respected Coach for standing firm. Several of the boys pleaded, "Come on, Coach. It was only one week when he had a bad grade. Can't we let him play? We'll work extra hard next week to help him with his math."

Wes interrupted them, "Guys, if we are going to play by the rules, then we have to play by all of them. I'm sorry I let you guys down, but I accept Coach's decision. I promise not to let you down again."

Ben appreciated Wes' position. This episode was going to be a hard lesson for them all.

Chapter 26

Franklin had won both of their first two games, so they were coming to Jordan with high expectations, especially since Jordan had lost both of their first two games. Ben hadn't told the team about the plans for Bobby to come to the game. He wanted that to be a surprise. As they got dressed for the game, a thought came to Ben, one of those things that only God could plant. Ben told the team, "After our initial warm ups, we'll re-group in the Bus Garage before the game begins."

Ben noted during warm ups that the Jordan crowd was significantly larger than the last two games. The newspaper had carried a small article about the close game at Gridley. Ben thought that may have helped. Regardless, he was glad to see a bigger crowd.

At the completion of warm ups they all went to the Bus Garage. Ben began, "I want to tell you a story. This is a story from the Bible, a true story. God was in the process of leading his people to the Promised Land, a place that would be much better for them. These people had been wandering in a desert for 40 years, because of their lack of faith. That was their punishment from God. But now, God was prepared to let them enter the Promised Land; however, they had to cross the Jordan River first. This was not a small feat, since the river was at flood stage. But as soon as the first priest stepped into the water, the water backed up, and all the people crossed the river bed without walking in water. As soon as everyone had crossed, God released the water and the river returned to flood stage. The people looked at the flooded river and realized there was no turning back. There was no option but to move on, and with God's help they did.

"I believe that we crossed the Jordan River with our last game. Now there is no turning back. We know what we are capable of and we know that we can play to honor God. So, now we move forward. After crossing the Jordan River, God's people had to do battle with many opponents. Joshua, their leader, directed them into each battle. There first opponent was Jericho, a well fortified city with a wall surrounding the entire perimeter. God told Joshua to have the people march in silence around the city. After seven days, the walls fell down and God's people defeated the people of Jericho.

"Tonight, when we go back out on the field, I want us to walk around the field. I want us to walk around the field in single file without saying a word. Marching won't make us victorious, but it will give all of us time to reflect on God's greatness and to meditate on how we can honor God tonight. When the Israelites marched around Jericho, the people of Jericho were terrified because they didn't know what was going to happen. Perhaps we can generate a feeling of uncertainty also. We need every advantage we can get!"

They re-entered the field with about 15 minutes before the kickoff. With Ben at the front of the line, they all marched in single file around the track which surrounded the football field. There was about 5 yards between each player. They marched without saying a word, all thinking about what had just happened earlier with Wes and how important the rules were that Coach was teaching them. Even more than before, they were realizing that these weren't rules on paper but rules with practical application. As they walked around the track, they suddenly detected an unusual silence in the crowd. No team had ever done this before. The players focused their attention straight ahead, but had they looked onto the field they would have seen opposing players with very uncertain looks in their eyes.

In the meantime George Baxter from the Jordan Chronicle made his way down from the crow's nest to the Jordan bench. He was waiting for Ben when they completed the lap around the track. "Mr. Harper, what is with no numbers on the jerseys? We can't tell who is running the football or who is making a tackle. You can't play football like this!"

One of the referees overheard the complaint by Mr. Baxter and interjected himself into the conversation. Ben recognized him as the referee he had talked to at the Gridley game. "Yes he can, Mr. Baxter. There is nothing in the Rule Book that requires players to have numbered jerseys."

Ben further commented, "If you recall, I asked you to not keep track of individual statistics for my players, but you refused. So, I had no other choice. I'm trying to generate team players, not individual heroes. I think you can report team statistics – that will be just fine."

A bit perturbed that he'd lost the battle, Mr. Baxter returned to the crow's nest realizing that Ben wasn't a typical coach.

With about two minutes before the kick-off, Ben called his team together into a huddle. As Ben was about to speak, Buck suddenly spoke up. "Coach, would you pray for us before we start the game? I think we really need God's guidance tonight."

Ben was surprised by Buck's request, but he appreciated the opportunity to pray with the boys. "Let's take off your helmets and get down on one knee. "Lord, I consider it a tremendous privilege to be the coach of these twelve young men. They are all very special to me. May you guide them and protect them in this game tonight. We know that only one team can win. The opponent wants to win as much as we do. Help us to accept whatever outcome you have planned. Help us to show love and kindness to our opponent, even if they don't show these things in return. Help us to honor you tonight in all that we say and do. Help our light to shine for you[12]. In Jesus name we pray, Amen."

"Alright boys, let's play football!" As they broke the huddle they noticed that Bobby was sitting in his wheelchair with his dad near the 50 yard line. "Coach, look!" they all shouted with

---

[12] Mat. 5:16 – "In the same way, let your light shine before others, that they may see your good deeds and glorify your Father in heaven." (NIV)

excitement. "It's Bobby." They all ran over and gave him a high five as they ran out to take their positions.

Bobby was all smiles as he cheered on his team. Ben walked over to Bobby and his dad. Ben gave Bobby a high five also. "Bobby, I'm so glad you could come tonight."

Bobby replied, "I heard you had something to do with that!"

"I think God had a bigger hand in it than I did. I was wondering if you could help me out tonight, sort of like being my assistant."

"Sure, Mr. Harper, that would be great, but what can I do?"

"Well," Ben said, "I have these big pieces of white cardboard with a number on each one. During the game, I may need you to hold up some of them for the players to see. I'll tell you which number to hold up and when. Do you think you can do that for me?"

"Sure, whatever you need."

After a few minutes of play, it appeared to Ben that the teams were fairly evenly matched, except of course that Jordan only had eleven players. The first quarter was back and forth with neither team making any great gains. At one point when Jordan had the ball, Ben noticed a little friction between his players and Franklin's players. Ben turned to Bobby and said, "Find No. 7 and hold it up high."

Bobby quickly sorted through the stack of boards and found No. 7. He held it up for all the players to see. As Jordan was huddling for the next play, Buck looked over to the sidelines and saw the No. 7 sign. Buck said, "Guys, look at Bobby, he is holding up No. 7."

"What is that supposed to mean?" Russ questioned.

124

"Rule No. 7, endure insults," Buck said. "Coach is telling us to change our attitudes. Remember last game? It was far worse than this and we endured. We can do it again." They all agreed and made a real effort to change. They began helping the other team players up after they had been tackled. They even complimented them on good plays.

The coaching assistant for Franklin saw the No. 7 sign also. He turned to the head coach and said, "Coach, I can't believe this, but Jordan is holding up play cards."

"Probably because they don't have anyone to run plays in, since they only have eleven players!" the coach chuckled. "Watch what play they run and we'll be ready next time! He really is a naïve coach!"

Jordan ran a play up the middle for a 10 yard gain. The assistant coach made a note on his clipboard – No. 7 fullback up the middle on the right side. He wouldn't forget. At another point, Ben had Bobby hold up No. 9. Ben's team immediately knew they needed to work hard on being team players. The assistant coach made another note on his clipboard.

At half time the score was 0 to 0. No one had scored, although Franklin had come close a couple of times. Quick thinking and team effort on Jordan's part saved a score on both occasions. By half time, the boys really needed a break. Losing one player was more of a physical strain than they had thought. But they were holding their own and had even threatened to score on one drive.

They retreated to the Bus Garage where they could have some privacy. They had a good discussion on what changes they needed to make, and how they needed to help each other out.

"Keep talking to each other," Ben said. "I have a feeling about this game – a feeling that we're going to pull off a victory." Ben didn't want to be too optimistic, since with only eleven players the odds were really against them. But somehow, he had a feeling.

They spent most of their time just resting. Before they went back out, Ben prayed for the boys again, that God would give them the strength to play hard, to play fair, and to honor God by their conduct.

The third quarter was much like the first half, a lot of back and forth with neither team able to make any great headway. Early in the fourth quarter, however, Franklin got close enough to the end zone that they were able to kick a field goal. That made the score 3 to 0 in favor of Franklin.

With only three minutes left in the game, Jordan got a break. Corky intercepted a pass and returned it to Franklin's 20 yard line. Ben suddenly noticed that Russ, who had been playing guard, was having trouble getting up. Ben and the others quickly ran to his aid. Russ had sprained his ankle when he was blocking for Corky. Now he could hardly walk. A couple of the boys helped Russ off the field. Now they would have to play with only ten players. They all knew this was going to be tough.

After the interception Ben heard some very derogatory comments from some of the Franklin players. Ben again told Bobby to hold up the No. 7 board. Though Ben's players didn't seem affected by the comments, Ben didn't think a reminder would hurt. The assistant coach for Franklin immediately picked up on the number card and told the head coach. "No. 7, that's the fullback up the middle on the right side."

The coach quickly instructed his players to push toward the middle. "We're going to stop them now," he barked to his team.

Ignorant that the Franklin coaches were trying to outsmart Jordan, Ben had Zeke call a down and out pass to the left side. All of the defensive line backers had prepared to crash the middle, so there was no one close to the wide receiver. The pass was complete and Jordan gained a first down. The assistant coach's face was almost red enough to be seen from the far side line. He was so positive that Ben was holding up play cards – now he had no idea what he was doing!

On the next play Ben had his team do the scramble play they ran during the previous game. All the players moved to some other position. They ran to the left side and gained four yards. It was second down and goal with only one minute left on the clock.

On the sidelines Russ was pleading with Ben to let him back in the game. "Coach, I can still play. My ankle feels a little better. I can at least fill a hole in the line."

Ben really wanted to put Russ back in the game also, but he didn't want to make things worse for Russ. "We need to wait, Russ. Let's see how it goes. We still have 60 seconds left."

Ben called a time out and ran out to meet his players in their huddle. "With only ten players we are at a severe disadvantage. They can pass rush before we can block all of them, so I think we will have to stay with our running plays. We have three chances to make six yards. We can do this!"

Ben still had one more time out to use, so he gave them two plays to run. "If we don't make a touchdown in two plays, call our last time out and we will re-group."

Jordan ran the first play, which was an end run on the right side. Franklin had it well covered and there was no gain on the play. The next play was a halfback run on the left side of the line, but again Franklin stopped them at the line of scrimmage. With only 20 seconds left in the game, Zeke called their last time out. Russ was still begging Ben to get back in the game. With a twinkle in his eye, Ben turned to Russ and said, "Do you think you can make it six yards?"

"Yeah, Coach, I'll do my best."

"OK, but stay here. I'll tell you my plan when I get back from the huddle."

Ben ran out to his team. "Gather around guys. This is what we are going to do. Zeke, I want you to run right, like we're going to attempt an end run again, except this time I want you to throw a pass back to Russ who will be standing just inside the sideline. Since he is injured, Franklin has assumed he is not playing, so he will be wide open for a pass. You will have to be fairly accurate with the pass because Russ won't be able to run after it. If he can make it six yards before they get to him, we'll have a touchdown. I don't want anyone to look over at Russ, otherwise we may give the play away. Any questions? OK, give me a few seconds on the sidelines to tell Russ what we are doing, then break huddle and proceed."

Buck chimed in, "OK guys, we can do this. Let's go!"

Ben appeared casual as he explained the plan to Russ. As the team approached the line of scrimmage, Ben had Russ step onto the field, but still appearing to be merely watching rather than playing. Ben took note that none of the Franklin players had picked up on the fact that Russ was on the field. The backfield referee was alert and saw that Russ was now a legitimate player, but fortunately he did not reveal anything to the opposing team.

The ball was snapped and Zeke took off full speed as though they were running a quarterback keeper around the right end. The entire Franklin team was rushing to the right side of the field. Suddenly Zeke stopped, looked over his left shoulder, and threw a perfect spiral to Russ on the opposite sideline. Russ caught the ball and started hobbling to the goal line. The nearest defender was fifteen yards away, but he was fast and had a chance of stopping Russ. At the one yard line the two players met. For Ben it was like a slow motion drama unfolding on TV. It seemed like it took Russ forever to cover the distance, and now the Franklin player was going to get him short of a touchdown. With his good leg Russ pushed hard and dove for the goal line. The Franklin player hit Russ hard and they both went down. When the referees got to the play, they declared it a touchdown, by inches. Ben hadn't taken a breath for what seemed like several minutes. Now his heart was racing. The whole team rushed over to help Russ and to congratulate him.

Ben had never seen them so happy. Even Bobby had stood up from his wheelchair and was yelling for his team.

The Franklin coach was furious. He called the referees over to the sideline screaming, "They can't do that. He wasn't even in the game!"

The referee calmly explained, "Coach, the boy was in bounds and on the line of scrimmage when the play was run. There is nothing illegal about the play." Turning away the coach was spewing profanities as he returned to the bench, profanities that no adult should hear, let alone a whole team of high school boys.

The extra point attempt failed, but that didn't seem to matter. The score was now 6 to 3 with only five seconds left on the clock. Jordan would have to kick-off. They had to hold them for one more play! Ben knew he could not put Russ in for the kick-off. He could barely walk, let alone run. With only five seconds remaining Ben knew Franklin's only chance of winning was to run the kickoff back for a touchdown. He felt their chances of stopping them were better if they went with an on-side kick. The guys would only have to run about ten yards and hopefully make the tackle.

The referee signaled for the kick-off to proceed. Sam kicked this time. It was a hard line drive that bounced just before the Franklin lineman. He was caught off guard, but managed to grab the ball. By that time Jordan was all over him. He didn't have a chance. The game was over! Jordan had won 6 to 3 -- their first victory in several years. All of the Jordan fans were celebrating. They came down on the field and congratulated the players. It was a happy time not just for the team but for the school and even the townspeople that had ventured out.

Chapter 27

Suddenly, Mr. Reed appeared in front of Ben. Ben had started picking up some of their paraphernalia along the sidelines and had not seen him coming. Ben noticed that he didn't seem to have the celebration spirit. Without any hesitation, Mr. Reed began his tirade. "Did I see you praying with the team before the game?"

"We did pray for a few minutes ---".

Before he could finish, Mr. Reed interrupted him. "That's what I thought. You can't just violate our school policy and expect to get away with it. I warned you about this when you started at Jordan High. The School Board meets Monday night at 7:00. I expect you to be there. Good night, Mr. Harper." That wasn't quite the speech Ben expected just after winning their first game. Now he didn't know what was going to happen.

The boys were jubilant after their first victory. Bobby even joined them for a few minutes in the locker room to tell them they all did a good job. He was always encouraging them. Ben was glad Bobby had been able to attend the game. Ben congratulated the team too, and praised them on a great team effort. He tried not to show his concern over his confrontation with Mr. Reed a few minutes earlier. He didn't want to spoil their joy.

Ben wrestled with his emotions most of the night. On one hand he was overjoyed at what the boys had accomplished, not just winning their first game, but really coming together as a team and helping one another both on and off the field. Now it appeared that Mr. Reed was throwing a wrench in the middle of all their progress. What would happen now?

Ben finally got up on Saturday morning and made some breakfast, although he wasn't very hungry. As he typically did on Saturday mornings, he made a trip to the store for some groceries. As he approached Ruth's house on his way, he saw her out in her yard tending her flowers, so he decided to stop. He really felt a need to talk to someone, and she always seemed to be a good listener. He pulled in her driveway and was met as always with her cheerful smile. "Hi, Ruth, your flowers look lovely. You must fertilize them every day."

"No, I just talk to them. They are good listeners, you know. They never talk back!"

A thought flashed into Ben's mind. "Flowers flourish when they listen to their master. We are all flowers in God's garden. We need to listen to our Master also."

Ruth interrupted his meditation. "I heard you won your football game last night! Congratulations! I'll bet the boys were thrilled over that."

"It was a great game. They played with a lot of heart. They've really come around as a team in the last couple weeks. "

Detecting some lack of enthusiasm in his voice, she said, "What's wrong, Ben? You don't seem quite like yourself."

"Well, last night as we were walking off the field, Mr. Reed rushed over and confronted me because I prayed with the boys just before the game began. He was furious and demanded that I attend the School Board meeting Monday night. Everything was going so well, but now I have no idea what will happen. It sure dampened the spirit of victory!"

"Did you explain that you weren't on school property when you prayed?"

"He didn't give me a chance to say anything. He just gave me his speech and then stomped off."

"You know, Ben, God has all kinds of reasons for the problems he brings our way. Maybe from God's perspective this isn't a problem but an opportunity. I'm confident that God will direct your path as you go through this. God doesn't let the righteous fall[13]."

"I always appreciate your insight, Ruth. Please pray for me Monday night. I'm sure I will need some extra help."

"No problem, Ben. I hope you have a good day." After Ben left, Ruth decided to make a call to her good friend Roger Dawson. She thought he might be able to provide some help for Ben.

For Ben Monday seemed like a very long day. He was having trouble getting engaged in his science classes, which was hardly ever a problem for him. Football practice went well, but he seemed to lack his normal motivation. Since the boys were doing so well, he didn't want to burden them with this new wrinkle.

After the locker room had cleared out, Ben headed home to freshen up and to get some supper before the meeting. He wasn't very hungry, but he knew he needed to eat a little to keep his stomach settled.

Roger was working around the Bus Garage when the boys left to go home from practice. Buck happened to walk past the garage and noticed Roger. They greeted each other as Buck approached. Roger congratulated Buck, "That was a great game Friday night. It is a real pleasure to see a team work together like you guys do. Keep up the good work!"

"Thanks," Buck said. "We've all been pretty excited, except Coach has seemed a little down since Friday night. That is not like him. He is usually upbeat all of the time."

"I heard he caught the wrath of Mr. Reed after the game because he prayed with you guys. Tonight he has to appear before

---

[13] Ps. 55:22 – Cast your cares on the Lord and he will sustain you; he will never let the righteous be shaken. (NIV)

the School Board at their meeting. I think he is a little worried about what might happen."

Buck was upset. "Coach is the best thing that has ever happened to us. He didn't do anything wrong."

"I know, Buck. Mr. Harper is a great guy. He really needs our support. I'm planning to attend the meeting tonight, just to be there for him."

Buck asked, "Is the meeting open to anyone?"

"Yes, it is a public meeting, so anyone can attend."

"Good," Buck said. "I'm going to see if I can get some of the other guys to attend also."

"That would be great, Buck! I'll see you there."

Buck hurried off and tried to catch up with some of the others.

Chapter 28

Ben arrived at the meeting a few minutes before 7:00 p.m. He took a seat in the second row of chairs that were set up for public attendees. Ben surveyed the board members and their name plates in front of them, but didn't recognize anyone. It made him wonder how involved they really were in the activities of the school. Mr. Reed was also at the table with the board members. There was no one else in the audience, except for one person just entering. Ben looked up and was surprised to see Roger coming through the door. Roger sat next to him and shook his hand as they greeted each other.

"Roger, what are you doing here?"

"A little messenger told me you might need some support tonight."

Before Ben could respond, the Board President, Mr. Phelps, pounded his gavel to begin the meeting. They started by going through some routine business, which was fine with Ben. He needed a few minutes to get his emotions adjusted anyway. Ben heard the door open again. He looked up and saw the entire football team walk in and take a seat a couple rows behind him. Ben wondered how they even knew about the meeting. He turned and quietly said, "What are you guys doing here?"

Buck replied, "We're a team, remember?"

Ben's heart was touched by the appearance of the team and by Buck's comment. They were indeed a team!

After about 30 minutes of regular business items, the President turned to Mr. Reed and asked, "Now, Mr. Reed, please explain to us the nature of your concern regarding Mr. Harper."

Mr. Reed seemed super energized as he began – like a cat toying with a mouse before it finally makes the kill. Ben silently prayed for God's help through this ordeal. "Mr. Harper is a new teacher at Jordan High this year. When he first arrived I clearly informed him that talking about God and praying anywhere on school property was strictly forbidden. Then, at Friday night's football game, what do I see? Before the opening kickoff, Mr. Harper huddles with the players on the field and prays with them. I'm certain he prayed because he confessed to it. In my book this is blatant disregard for the school's rules and demands immediate discipline. If the faculty members are allowed to break the rules, what kind of a message does that send to the students? There will be no order of any kind. My recommendation is that Mr. Harper be terminated from coaching football immediately."

Ben's jaw must have dropped three inches when he heard Mr. Reed's recommendation. He never expected this outcome. He was in shock. Had he turned around, he would have seen a similar reaction from the entire team. They all knew it would be the end of their football season if the board carried out Mr. Reed's recommendation.

After what seemed like an eternal pause, the Board President finally spoke. "Mr. Reed, this is a very serious recommendation you are presenting to us. Is this the only incident of misconduct or have you have observed other situations also?"

At the game Friday night they did some kind of parade around the field before the game started. I'm not sure what that was all about, but it was just weird. It is certainly unconventional for our team to act like that. The team is also playing with jerseys that don't have any numbers on them. I know there are a lot of jerseys left over from last year that could be used. It is impossible to even tell who is playing. That is totally uncalled for and unnecessary."

"Is Mr. Harper in the audience tonight?" the President asked.

Ben stood up and said, "I'm Ben Harper."

"Mr. Harper, you've obviously heard the accusations by Mr. Reed. The most alarming to us is conducting prayer on the football field, which is a violation of school policy and has significant consequences. The other things Mr. Reed mentioned are perhaps unorthodox, but they are not as significant as the prayer issue. Do you have any comments that you would like to make?"

"Yes, Mr. President. I would like to make a statement. I became a teacher because I love kids. I especially love to teach high school students because I know the transition from childhood to adulthood is very difficult. It is very easy for kids in this transition period to get on the wrong path, which may impact them for the rest of their lives. My goal is to help them find the right path, the path that will help them live by a higher standard than the rest of the world. I believe that if I fail at this, then I have failed as a teacher. I confess that I do some unconventional things in my classes and on the football field, but it is only to stimulate the students to get excited about learning and to excel at what they do.

"I began teaching at Jordan High this past spring. I came as a science teacher. Coaching football wasn't even on my radar screen. It wasn't until I was approached by a group of boys that really wanted to play football that I got involved. I have no experience as a football coach or any type of coaching for that matter. I started to play football in high school, but injured my knee, which ended my football career. I agreed to coach these boys because I felt it would be a good way for them to learn the principles of character and conduct that would benefit them not only on the football field but in all of life.

"We walk around the football field before a game so that we can better focus on the things we need to do – to play with the right attitude, to play as a team and not as individuals, to be kind to our opponent, and in all things to honor God with our words and conduct. The jerseys without numbers were donated, so there was no cost to the school. I recognized after our first game that when the announcer highlights an individual for a good play or when the media publishes individual statistics, team performance suffers and individual performance is elevated. If one player scores, it is usually because the other ten players made it possible. Therefore, it is a team score and not an individual score. The media and announcers were not willing to comply with my request to not announce individual statistics, so I made it happen another way. Since doing this, the boys have really played much better as a team.

"On my first day in Jordan I met with Mr. Reed and he explained the rule that I could not talk about God or pray with the students on school property. I have not done either of these things in my classroom or anywhere in school. I did pray with the team on the football field Friday night before the game began, but since the football field is not school property, I didn't think I did anything wrong."

The School Board President immediately interrupted Ben. "What do you mean the football field is not school property? It is part of our school campus and has been since the school was first built."

Roger quickly raised his hand to speak. "Mr. Dawson, I gather you have some thoughts on this issue?"

"I do, Mr. President. I think I can clarify this issue. When the school was first built, my father sold the land to the School District so they could build the school. However, the School District did not have enough money at the time to also purchase land for the football field. My dad was a sports enthusiast and didn't want to see the school not have a football field. So, he prepared an agreement with the School District whereby they could lease the property for $1000 per year and construct whatever facilities they needed. They accepted the agreement and built the football field and the Bus Garage. Therefore, since the beginning the school has merely leased the property. When my father passed away, I inherited his possessions. I had no desire to change anything, so the lease agreement is still in effect. I know that board members change over time, so it is understandable that you might not know this. I have a copy of the lease agreement right here if anyone would like to see it. So, Mr. Harper is correct. He was not on school property when he prayed with the team."

The President responded, "Well, this is certainly surprising news to most of us, if not all of us."

Mr. Reed blurted out, "It is ridiculous, that's what it is. It was still a school function, regardless."

There was a period of awkward silence and then Buck stood up. "Young man, do you wish to address the Board?"

"Yes, I would. My name is Buck and I'm one of the football players."

"Are these other fellows some of your teammates?" the President asked.

"Yes, sir, these are *all* of my teammates."

The President paused as he was obviously counting heads. "There are only twelve players on your team! How can you play football with only twelve players?"

Buck calmly responded, "It only takes eleven, sir. We have a spare."

After a bit of a chuckle from the other Board members, the President said, "OK, what do you want to say?"

"In years past our football teams were really bad. I know because I was part of the recent ones. Our only goal was to be macho. We all had big egos and only wanted personal glory. At the end of last year, as you know, the school terminated the football program. Over the summer a bunch of us realized how much we still wanted to play, even though our attitudes still hadn't changed much. We pleaded with Mr. Harper to be our coach and to see if the school would reconsider and allow us to have a team again. I'm not sure how Coach Harper did it, but he was able to get permission for us to play. From the very beginning we realized that Coach Harper really cares about us, not just how we play as football players, but how we act as students and how we live as adults. No other coach has ever been that concerned about us nor given us so much help. He is the best thing that has happened to us in a very long time.

"When he prayed on the football field the other night, it was because I asked him to pray. He didn't pray for God to help us score a bunch of points, or that we would win the game. He prayed that we would play with right attitudes, that we would show kindness to our opponent, that we wouldn't get upset when we are insulted, stuff like that. His prayer really helped us to stay focused on the right things. All of us have made huge improvements in our conduct and in our grades because of Coach Harper. I confess that before Coach Harper came to Jordan High I was one of the biggest bullies in school, but not anymore. Most of us were barely passing our classes, but not anymore. We are doing good work now because he helps us and cares about us. Please don't terminate Coach Harper. That would be devastating to all of us."

"Buck, thank you for your comments," the President said. "It is certainly commendable that you can even play football with only twelve players. And it is commendable that you have such high regard for Mr. Harper."

The interchange was interrupted when another Board member began to speak. "I question Mr. Harper's method of recruiting players. My son wanted to play this year, but he said each person had to commit to maintaining a 'C' average in all classes. School policy only requires a passing grade for students to play extracurricular activities. Why, Mr. Harper, are you arbitrarily taking it upon yourself to limit those who can play? I think that is showing favoritism, which cannot be tolerated!"

Ben hadn't expected this new accusation in this "condemnation" process. He maintained his composure, but he sensed things were getting out of hand. "When I first met with Mr. Reed, not only did he tell me about the God/prayer issue, but he also made it quite clear that every student was expected to pass, and as he said, whatever it takes. Honestly, that is not my philosophy at all. I don't believe that as a teacher I'm merely here to crank parts out the door. If that is truly what you want, then I'm not the teacher you want in your school and I'm not the coach you want for these boys.

"I've told all of my students that the grade you get is the grade you earn. I expect hard work and dedicated effort. I've told them many times that if they need help I'm more than willing to meet with them in study hall or after school, and many students have come forward and asked for assistance. I believe that most students can do much better than what they think, if only they apply themselves and are given a little encouragement.

"I did implement the 'C' standard because I feel it is a privilege for any student to participate in extracurricular activities. These students become role models for the other students; therefore, they need to live by a higher standard. If a student isn't willing to commit to this, then I'm concerned that they may not set a good example for the other students to follow.

"After almost every practice we have a study time in the locker room where the boys help each other with homework assignments they might be struggling with in school. I'm there to help also. Because of their commitment and our study time together, their grades have improved tremendously, and they are truly excited about learning. By helping each other with school work, they are learning the benefit of teamwork. Because they work as a team when they are studying, they also play as a team on the football field. They need each other. This is a principle they can take with them the rest of their lives. So, if promoting a good thing is wrong, then I am guilty!"

After another uncomfortable pause, the President spoke. "Mr. Harper, it sounds like you have good intentions and have accomplished many good things, but in light of what we've heard tonight about prayer on the football field, it sounds like you are stretching, if not violating, our school rule even though the football field is technically not owned by the school. If we allow this to continue, it opens the door for every coach and teacher to do whatever they want, potentially creating chaos. We just can't let that happen. It also jeopardizes our State funding if we fail to comply with State requirements, and no prayer in school is one of their requirements. Therefore, I believe we have no option but to take disciplinary action. Does anyone on the Board have a contrary opinion?"

Looking around at the other Board members, the President didn't see anyone opposing his contention. It was becoming obvious to Ben that most of the Board members were "yes" men to the President – unwilling to speak their own mind. Ben realized that things were not boding well for him. Before his mind realized what his body was doing, Ben jumped to his feet.

"Mr. President, before you do what I think you are going to do, I would like to say that these boys have worked very hard and they have really come together as a team. I really don't think it would be good for them to cut their season short. That would be a huge discouragement to them. I ask that you let me continue to coach as I have been doing until the end of the season. If at that time you don't see a big improvement in the boys' attitude, conduct, and grades, then I will resign my position not only as coach but as teacher also."

Looking a bit pensive, the President responded, "Well, that is a gutsy offer, Mr. Harper. Are you sure you want to risk your teaching position by gambling on these guys?"

"Well, Mr. President, I would be willing to risk my life for any of these boys, so I guess my teaching position is no big deal!"

"This really doesn't make sense to me. Mr. Harper, all you have to do to resolve this problem is to stop praying on the football field. Is that such a big deal?"

"Yes, Mr. President, it is a big deal to me. After all that God has done for me, I cannot yield to your request. I am willing to make the sacrifice I've offered[14]."

"Very well. Is there any discussion from the Board members before we entertain a motion? Seeing none, do I have a motion?"

Ben was holding his breath and silently praying that the Board would let him continue. Finally one of the board members spoke up. "I don't agree with some of the things that Mr. Harper has done, but I admire his commitment to these boys. I make a motion that we allow Mr. Harper to finish the season as the football coach, and then the Board will decide whether to terminate his employment or not."

The President asked, "Is there any discussion on the motion?" There were no comments. "OK, then, all in favor say I."

The vote was unanimous. "Mr. Harper, the Board will re-evaluate your performance and make our determination at the end of the season."

"Thank you," Ben said. "Now the burden is on each of you to objectively observe these boys over the next few weeks to determine if prayer on the football field is a detriment to them. I also challenge you to check their grades, to talk to their teachers, to observe them at school and when they are not at school, to attend their football games and see how they conduct themselves on the field. I hope that you will be faithful and follow through with your end of the deal. Thank you."

---

[14] Rom. 12:1-2 – Therefore, I urge you brothers, in view of God's mercy, to offer your bodies as a living sacrifice, holy and pleasing to God – this is your true and proper worship. Do not conform to the pattern of this world, but be transformed by the renewing of your mind. (NIV)

Ben, Roger, and the boys all left the room and congregated for a few minutes in the parking lot. "Thank you, Roger, for attending tonight and for your support through this ordeal," Ben said.

"No problem," Roger replied. "You are still welcome to use the Bus Garage any time you want. I have to get home, but I'll be praying for all of you. Don't give up doing what's good!"

"Thanks, Roger. We'll catch you later," Ben said as Roger hurried to his car.

Zeke was the first of the boys to speak. "So, what do we do now, coach?"

"God is in control of all things. He has a purpose even in this episode tonight. We may not know what it is, but we need to trust Him. We are going to keep doing what we've been doing. I believe that we are doing what God wants us to do. So, we continue. Thank you guys for coming tonight, but I am, curious. How did you even know about the meeting?"

Buck said, "I happened to see Mr. Dawson after practice tonight and he told me about it. I got in touch with everyone else and we all decided that a team should stick together."

"Thanks," Ben responded. "It was great to see all of you guys walk in tonight. I'm sure you surprised the School Board members! You guys have a good night. I'll see you all at school tomorrow. Keep praying!"

Just as Ben walked in his door at home, his phone began to ring. It was Ruth. "Ben, I saw you pull in your driveway. I couldn't wait any longer to find out how the meeting went."

"Well," Ben said, "it was far more intense than what I expected." He continued to tell Ruth the whole story.

"That is the way Satan works," Ruth said. "When you start to do something good, he tries to direct your steps off the path. Stand firm, Ben. God blesses those who honor Him[15]. I'll keep praying for you."

"Thanks, Ruth. I need all the help I can get right now."

When Ben finally went to bed, he was sure it was going to be a long night. His mind was racing at 100 miles an hour. Suddenly, he felt all the tension of the evening fade away. He closed his eyes and was instantly asleep.

---

[15] I Sam. 2:30b – ,,, "Those who honor me I will honor, but those who despise me will be disdained." (NIV)

Chapter 29

The next morning the sun was bright and warm. There was a gentle breeze and the birds were singing with joy. The flowers were open and bright. The grass was bright green and still glistening with dew drops. It was a clear reminder that Ben didn't need to worry about the day[16]. God would take care of it and every other day to come, just like he had taken care of all the past days. Ben knew he was ready for whatever the day would bring. He collected his things and hurried to school.

Ben seemed to teach even more fervently than normal, if that were possible. Even the students could sense more intensity than usual. It was contagious. They were energized to study and work together even more than before.

Football practice went well after school. No one said much about the previous evening, but they all knew very well what was on the line – Coach Harper's job!

Their next opponent was Danvers. They were nearly an equal match to Jordan, except for having 20 more players than Jordan. But, that was typical for every team they played.

Danvers was an away game, so on Friday night they packed up their equipment in several cars and drove 45 minutes to Danvers. As Ben expected, the Jordan crowd was rather sparse, although a few more students were in the stands than at the previous away game. He was glad to see that. He wished, too, that Bobby could have come, but it was the doctor's orders that he stay close to the hospital in case something changed quickly. Ben had to admit that

---

[16] Mat. 6:25, 33 – "Therefore I tell you, do not worry about your life, what you will eat or drink; or about your body, what you will wear. Is not life more than food, and the body more than clothes? But seek first his kingdom and his righteousness, and all these things will be given to you as well." (NIV)

he did like having Bobby on the sidelines with him. His presence seemed to bring greater motivation to Ben and the team.

When Jordan entered the football field, they once again marched around the track in total silence before they went through their warm up drills. Right before the game, Ben huddled the team together and they prayed. Ben knew this might ultimately be his demise, but he also knew that changing his principles to merely satisfy the School Board could have even greater consequences in God's eyes. Serving God was a much higher priority than serving the School Board.

Both teams played good football. Danvers initiated a couple confrontations during the game, but Jordan handled them with poise. They didn't retaliate in any way. Their lack of response seemed to silence their opponent. Jordan broke free for a couple long runs during the game and they were able to hold off Danvers' closing rally to win 19 to 14.

Ben and the boys were ecstatic. They now had two wins in a row! There was much joyful celebration as they all joined together on the field. They were truly a team. Ben was thankful.

Ben was hopeful that the team would get some recognition in the Saturday newspaper, since they had played a good game. There was indeed a small article buried in the sports section. It was titled "Jordan Football – Longest Winning Streak in 5 Years." The article essentially insinuated that Jordan had gotten lucky and that the rest of the season would undoubtedly end as the previous ones had. Unfortunately, that seemed to be the attitude of a lot of people in town. Ben hoped the boys didn't see the article. He didn't want them to be discouraged after playing so well. Ben knew they had a mountain to climb, and he wasn't going to give up.

The boys stopped by Bobby's house over the weekend to fill him in on the game. He was anxious as always to hear every detail. Bobby was getting stronger day by day. Everyone was glad to see that. When the boys left, Bobby started talking to his mom and dad. "I wish there was something special I could do for the team."

"What are you thinking?" his mom asked.

"I don't know for sure. They have helped me so much. I would like to help them in return."

"I have an idea," Bobby's dad said. "You like to paint, right?"

"Yeah."

"Maybe we can surprise them."

"But how?"

Bobby's dad explained his idea. They all thought it was a great plan.

Game 5 on Friday night was against Alento. Ben didn't know much about this team either, except their record was 3 and 1 overall and 2 and 0 in the conference. They would be a challenge, just like every other opponent. Ben's classes were going well and the boys were doing well with their grades. The group study sessions after practice seemed to have helped tremendously. Ben hadn't seen or heard from any of the School Board members since the meeting, so he wasn't sure if they were even paying any attention to the boys. He knew he couldn't worry about that – it was in God's hands.

Thursday night after football practice Bobby's dad made arrangements with the janitor to let he and Bobby into the locker room once everyone had left. For Bobby it was like a secret mission. He was excited. They collected each player's helmet and labeled them with a piece of paper so they could keep track of which helmet belonged to each player.

They took the helmets home and placed them on a piece of large plastic on the garage floor. The helmets were badly scuffed and marred. Previous attempts to clean them had only been partially successful. Bobby's dad had picked up some heavy duty paint from the hardware store, so they could repaint the helmets. They sanded out the scratch marks first and then cleaned them with soap and water. After they dried, they applied a thick coat of red gloss paint. The thick paint covered all the blemishes very well. When they finished the helmets looked almost new. To finish the process they painted the letter "I" for Indians on each side of each helmet.

Bobby was overjoyed. "Dad, they look great! I hope the guys will be surprised."

"I'm fairly certain that none of them will be expecting this," his dad replied.

"How are we going to get them back without anyone seeing us?"

"We'll take them back early tomorrow evening before the game begins."

On Friday about 5:00 Bobby and his dad packed all the newly painted helmets in a couple large boxes and drove back to the school. Since the helmets were in boxes, if someone saw them they wouldn't be able to tell what they were carrying.

The janitor again met them at the locker room and unlocked the door. He also agreed to stand guard for a few minutes while Bobby and his dad unpacked the boxes. Bobby's dad took each helmet out of the box and handed it to Bobby. Bobby checked the number they had taped inside and then set the helmet on the bench in front of the appropriate locker. He lined them all neatly in a row. Undoubtedly the guys would see them as soon as they entered the locker room. Bobby wished he could hide in the corner and see their eyes when they came in, but he knew he couldn't. Hopefully, he would hear about it later.

Bobby and his dad quickly picked up their boxes and thanked the janitor for his help on the way out. Now it was time to go home and get ready for the game. On the drive home, Bobby turned to his dad and said, "Thank you, Dad. That was a good idea. I'm glad we could do this together!"

Bobby's dad looked at his son and said, "That is what team work is all about!"

Ben got to the locker room a little early. He had several things on his mind and wasn't really paying attention as he entered the room. Then he sensed a smell of fresh paint. Odd, he thought. Who would have been painting in here? When he rounded the corner to where the lockers were, he saw 12 perfectly painted red helmets sitting in a line on the bench. At first he thought the helmets were new, but the paint smell confirmed that they had been repainted. He couldn't imagine who had done this.

After all they had been through in the last week or so, Ben was thrilled to think that someone was willing to help the team in this way. He couldn't wait for the boys to come in and see the surprise.

About a half hour later, the boys arrived. Rob was the first one around the end of the lockers. As soon as he saw the helmets he yelled, "Hey guys, we got new helmets!" They all rushed over to take a look. After a more detailed investigation, they realized they weren't new, but painted. They were filled with excitement.

Zeke said, "Coach, did you do this?"

"No I didn't, but somebody must really like you guys to go to all this work!"

"They look great," Buck said.

Tommy commented, "The helmets even have an 'I' for Indians painted on each side."

Ben replied, "Since there is an 'I' on each side, we should think of this as 'Indians of integrity'."

"Yeah," Corky said. "I like that. Rule #1 – we are men of integrity."

That act of kindness was like an energy boost for the boys. They were all enthused about having something new. And the letter "I" was a constant reminder to live with integrity.

The boys all got dressed and ran onto the field proudly sporting their refurbished helmets. As they started their warm up exercises, Ben glanced around the stands and realized that the home crowd was larger than last week. There were more students and adults both. It certainly helped to see more fans and to hear them cheering. Ben occasionally glanced into the bleachers to see if any Board members were present, but without staring, it was hard to make any definite identification. The team did their silent walk around the field before the game, which was now becoming a tradition. Ben also prayed again with the team on the field before the game began.

Chapter 30

The game against Alento was another hard fought game, but Jordan capitalized on a couple breaks and won by a score of 12 to 7. That boosted their conference record to 3 and 0, an unbelievable run for Jordan, considering their past seasons and their small team.

After the game, each Jordan player politely shook the hand of every player on the Alento team as well as the coaches and referees. Ben noticed that some of the boys even spent a few minutes talking to some of the Alento players. They were truly trying to be kind to their opponents.

On their way back to the locker room they also filed down the sideline and gave Bobby a high five. He had been there again and was all smiles as the boys came over to greet him. He couldn't resist commenting on their helmets. "Hey, I like your new helmets! They really make you stand out!"

By the smile on Bobby's face and the twinkle in his eye, Buck made an educated guess. "Did you have anything to do with this?"

Keeping a secret was not Bobby's specialty. With excitement he confessed. "Me and my dad painted them. We wanted to surprise all of you."

"Well you certainly did that," Buck said. "That was one of the best surprises ever!" With that Buck and Tommy hoisted Bobby up on their shoulders and carried him off the field. Bobby was thrilled. He felt like he was one of the team. In a sense, he really was becoming one of them. His inspiration had been crucial in the success the boys were enjoying.

There was starting to be a little buzz around town as well as at school that the football team was doing well this year, much better than the last several years and much better than expected. There seemed to be more excitement in the air. Ben was encouraged by what he was seeing and hearing. He hoped the School Board members were paying attention.

Tuesday was the traditional "Art Day" at Jordan High. The art class in particular had numerous projects on display throughout the school for teachers and students to observe. Tuesday evening there was an art open house, a time when anyone in the school or community could meander through the school and see all the various projects the students had completed. Ben always made an effort to attend things like this to show his interest in the students and hopefully to encourage them. He talked with many of his science students who were displaying projects. He was impressed with their skills and he complimented many students throughout the evening.

At one end of the hallway he noticed a painting of an old red barn neatly trimmed in white with a majestic oak tree nearby. There was an eagle soaring against the floating clouds in the distance. Ben really liked the picture because it seemed to portray an image of peace. He was so engulfed in the painting that he hadn't noticed Anne from his science class standing a few feet away.

"Hi, Anne," Ben said. "This is a beautiful painting. You are very talented!"

"Thanks, Mr. Harper. I enjoy doing it. It helps me relax. I heard about your meeting with the School Board the other night."

"How did you find out about that?"

"Some of the boys told us. I'm glad you are taking a stand, Mr. Harper. I think what you've accomplished since you've been at Jordan is incredible. I've been in high school for four years and I've never seen the kids as positive as they are now. I can tell that you really care about your students. We really appreciate that. You are making a difference, even if the School Board doesn't agree with what you are doing. Though I graduate this year, I really hope you don't have to leave. It would be a huge loss for our school."

"Thank you for your kind words, Anne. Sometimes doing what is right is not always the most popular thing, but I know that our Creator (I have to watch what I say, you know) is in control and that He is working out His plan, even though that is hard for us to understand sometimes.

"Say, I just had a thought. Would you be willing to do a favor for me?"

"What would you like me to do?"

"Well, I've been really stressing team work with the football players and they have picked it up very well. If I cut out a large football shape on a piece of plywood, could you paint it like a football, but with twelve puzzle pieces on it? And then could you paint each player's name on one piece of the puzzle? I want to hang it up in the locker room as a reminder that it takes every player to make the team complete. If even one piece is missing, we can't function properly."

"That sounds like a really great idea. I'd be happy to paint it. It shouldn't be too difficult."

"Thanks, Anne. I'll try and get it to you tomorrow!"

Anne completed the football painting and returned it to Ben on Friday after school. "Wow, Anne, this looks great!" The football was perfectly painted with the white laces and twelve puzzle pieces, each outlined in yellow and each being a different shape. Across each piece was the name of each player boldly painted with red letters. In taller letters she had painted the word "INDIANS" in the spaces between each lace.

It was better than Ben had imagined. "Thanks so much, Anne. I'm going to hang this up right now before our game tonight."

"I'm glad I could help, Mr. Harper. Thanks for asking me. It feels good to be able to contribute to the team."

Ben covered the football with a large garbage bag so none of the players would see it before the game, although most of them had left after school and would be returning later. Ben hung the football on the open wall above the chalk board, a place where everyone would be reminded of how important they were to the team.

Ben went home to get a bite to eat and then returned to get ready for the game. At first no one saw the football because it was hanging above the chalk board. Suddenly, Jimmy exclaimed, "Hey look guys!"

They all looked up and saw the football with its twelve puzzle pieces. There was silence for a few minutes as they all pondered the puzzle and its meaning. Sam finally broke the silence. "If one piece is missing the puzzle is not complete. We all have to work together for the team to function properly."

"You're exactly right," Ben said. This is the best example I could think of to symbolize team effort. You are all different sizes and you all have different abilities, but when all of you are put together, you fit perfectly into one team. May it be a reminder that we are one team, not twelve players."

"This is a great idea, Coach," Zeke said. "Did you make this?"

"I cut the board, but Anne from my science class painted it for us."

"Wow!" Zeke said. "She did a really nice job."

"You should all thank her if you get a chance," Ben said.

Chapter 31

They all got ready for their game against Parksville. From what Ben could learn Parksville was not always at the top of the conference, but they were rarely at the bottom. This year was no exception. They'd had a few bumps in the road, but they were doing well and their team was healthy.

The Jordan crowd was growing larger each week. Ben thought the crowd for this home game was larger than last week's. A cheering crowd always helped inspire the boys. Bobby was on the sidelines, as usual for home games with his number signs ready. He took his job seriously. Ben appreciated his dedication and enthusiasm. This little boy had done more for the team than anything Ben could do. Ben thought it's amazing how that works!

The first half ended with Jordan leading 18 to 16. About half way through the third quarter Ben heard someone yelling on the sidelines behind him. He turned to see Bobby laying on the ground and his dad next to him yelling for help. Since there was a lot of commotion going on, the referee stopped the game. Ben hurried over to Bobby. He had passed out and had fallen off the bench. He was no longer using a wheelchair because over the past few weeks he had gotten a lot stronger. He had been doing very well with no complications since the bone marrow transplant. The ambulance was on the way. Fortunately he was still breathing, but was unresponsive.

The whole Jordan team gathered around Bobby to see what had happened. While they were waiting for the EMTs to arrive, Ben suggested that they pray for Bobby. They formed a circle around Bobby and his parents. Bobby's mom had been in the bleachers, but she came running onto the field as soon as she saw what had happened. The whole team took off their helmets and got down on one knee. Ben prayed, "Lord, we don't understand what is happening to little Bobby. He has been doing so well. We know that you love him and we pray that you will take care of him. He is our friend, Lord. Please heal him if it is your will."

Just then the ambulance entered the gate at the south end of the football field and was backing up to where Bobby was laying. They quickly loaded him into the ambulance with his parents and rushed off to the hospital.

Ben tried to regroup the boys. "Just remember, God has a plan for Bobby's life. We don't know what that is, but God does and He is in complete control. Let's try and stay focused on the game. Maybe afterwards we can go see him at the hospital."

"We'd like that, Coach," Buck said.

The rest of the game was a bit of a struggle. They all loved Bobby. Not seeing him on the sidelines was hard, especially knowing that he might be seriously ill. There was a couple times during the remainder of the game when Parksville nearly scored, but Jordan was able to hold them off. The game finally ended with Jordan on top 18 to 16. It was a huge win for Jordan, now 4 and 0 in the conference, but that didn't seem too important now with Bobby's health in jeopardy again.

The boys rushed to get dressed and then they all headed to the hospital. They inquired at the front desk and learned that Bobby was on the same floor as he was previously. They all crowded into the elevator. Fortunately it was a big elevator. As they exited the elevator, Ben saw Mrs. Green, the head nurse, at the nurse's station. She knew immediately why they were there. "The doctor tried Bobby on a new medication this week," she said. "Everything was going well until this evening. It appears that Bobby had a reaction to the medicine. He is awake now and stable. We plan to keep him over night, but he should be able to go home in the morning."

"So, he is going to be OK?" Buck asked.

"Yes, once the medicine gets out of his system, he should be just fine."

"That is great news," Ben said. "We are all relieved. Can we go see him for a few minutes?"

"That should be OK. I would just ask that you not stay too long, since he is very tired."

Ben and the boys headed down the hallway to Bobby's room, anxious to see him. As soon as they walked through the door, Bobby's eyes lit up. "You came to see me!"

"Of course," Zeke said, "we had to check up on our most favorite fan."

"Did you win tonight?" Bobby asked anxiously.

"We did," Buck said. "It was 18 to 16. It was close, but we held on."

"I knew it. I knew it. I knew it!" Bobby said. "You guys are the greatest!"

Ben observed that Bobby was more concerned about the team than he was about his own health. They only stayed a few minutes as the nurse had requested. Bobby's parents thanked them several times for coming. Bobby thanked them too. They were all greatly relieved as they left the hospital and walked out into the parking lot.

"I'm glad we came tonight," Cody said.

"Yeah, me too," Russ chimed in.

"It is great to know that Bobby is going to be alright," Ben said. "Hey, would you guys like to come over to my house tomorrow night? I can build a bonfire and maybe we can roast some hot dogs."

"That sounds great, Coach," Zeke said. "I'd love to come." All the others eagerly agreed, as well.

"Let's say around 6:00 p.m. at my house. I'll see you all then."

Chapter 32

Ben had some old firewood in the back yard that had been stacked there for several years from the way it looked. He carried it to the side yard where there was a natural dip in the terrain. It would make a great place for a bonfire. Ben went to the grocery store in the early afternoon and stocked up on hot dogs, chips, marshmallows, condiments, and soft drinks. He had no idea how much food it would take to satisfy twelve hungry football players. He tried to plan on the high side, but there was still a shadow of doubt in his mind.

Ben started the fire late afternoon so that it would be ready when everyone came. Ben had been with these boys every day, except weekends, for several weeks – ever since football practice began. He was well acquainted with all of them, but tonight he had an anxious feeling for some reason. He had no idea why he was feeling the way he was.

All of the boys showed up right on time. Ben had set up a table near the bonfire, and several of the boys helped him carry the food out to the table. Ben had previously cut some sticks to use for roasting hot dogs, so everything was ready to go. After offering a brief prayer, he told the boys to help themselves. There was no hesitation on the part of anyone. They were all hungry. Ben was glad to see them together and having fun with each other.

They finally got filled up and were just enjoying time around the fire. It was a clear night. The stars were shining bright. The air was crisp, which made the fire feel good. There was something about a bonfire at night that caused people to talk about things they normally wouldn't reveal. There was a moment when everyone was quiet, one of those moments when all conversations seem to end at the same time.

Buck was the one who finally broke the silence. "Hey, Zeke, where did you learn to throw a football like you do? You know, not end over end, but kind of a wobbly spiral."

Everyone laughed. Then with a slight smirk on his face, Zeke replied. "When I was in grade school, we were very poor. My dad had trouble holding a job and consequently we didn't have money for extras like a football. We kids always spent the summers with my grandma and grandpa on their farm. We helped them with their garden stuff. Once in a while Grandpa would let us play catch with a cantaloupe or small watermelon. Of course, once you dropped it a few times, it got pretty mushy. I guess I never got used to seams on the ball! I think Grandpa is still working on that hybrid!" When Zeke finished, he said, "OK Buck, now it is your turn to enlighten us with a secret story from your past."

Buck hesitated for several seconds, swallowed hard, and then said, "My story is not as mushy as throwing cantaloupe!" The others all laughed again. "One day when I was about two years old, according to my mom, my dad left the house one morning and never came back. Their marriage wasn't going well, and so he thought life would be better if he just went away. The only thing I remember about my dad is when he climbed into his old pickup truck and drove off. I never saw him again. I can't even remember what he looked like.

"When my dad left, it was up to my mom to take care of me. She had to work extra hours just to make ends meet. Consequently, I was always staying with someone – grandparents, relatives, and friends. I didn't see my mom much because she was always working. As I got older I began to resent what my dad did to our family. I was bitter. I was angry. I was jealous of other kids that had a dad and a full time mom. I felt like I didn't really have a home. My feelings caused me to get in trouble at school. I didn't respect my teachers or other students. I was a big bully! Most kids didn't like me, which was fine. I didn't like them either. If it hadn't been for Coach and this football team, I hate to think where my life would have ended up. But I know now that God has a plan for my life, and I need to follow Him. Sorry that I've not been the best of friends to all of you in years past. I'm working hard to change that now. I thank you for being friends to me. It means so much to me."

After another moment of silence as the group processed what Buck had just revealed, Buck said to Jimmy who was sitting next to him, "I think I had better quit. Jimmy, it is your turn now."

And so for the next hour the boys all shared their stories one by one. Some of the stories were happy ones and some were sad. But everyone had a story to tell. When all of the boys had finished, there was a time of quiet reflection. Each was pondering what the others had said. They learned things about each other that were drawing them closer together as friends, as teammates. Buck broke the silence again and said, "Coach, what is your story? Why did you come to Jordan? With your teaching ability you could have taught in any school in the country!"

Ben, too, hesitated for a very long moment and then decided that it was time to share his story with all of them. "Before I came here, my wife and I taught at a school in Cleveland, Ohio. "

"Wait a minute, Coach. You are married?" Corky asked with a puzzled look on his face.

"I *was* married. Amy, my wife, and I met in college during our junior year. It was sort of love at first sight. We were both studying to be teachers, so we had a lot of classes together. We dated until we graduated, then we got married. We both got jobs in the same school district. She was a grade school teacher and I was a high school science teacher. We both loved our jobs. We loved teaching and helping kids.

"We rented a small house a few miles from our schools. We each had to drive separately because the grade school and the high school were not very close together. We were in our third year of teaching. Everything was going well. Classes in the high school started earlier than in the grade school, so I always left home earlier than Amy.

"One morning in late September, just over a year ago, the weather was gorgeous. It was a bright sunny day. The air was slightly cool, but refreshing. During my first hour science class I was called out of my room by the Principal. He informed me that Amy had been involved in a car accident not far from our house. I quickly rushed to the scene of the accident to see the medics loading Amy into the ambulance, but she was in a black bag that was zipped shut. I knew instantly that she was gone," Ben said, fighting back the tears. "It was really no one's fault. An elderly man suffered a severe heart attack and passed out as he entered the intersection my wife was driving through. He was unable to stop at the red light. He hit her car broadside on the driver side door. My wife was killed instantly. That was the hardest day of my life. In a split second, life changed forever.

"I took about a week off from school for the funeral and to go through some of her things. But being at home with all of those constant reminders was harder than working. So, I went back to school and resumed teaching. But that was difficult too, because no one knew what to say to me. People seemed glad that I was back, but for the most part they ignored talking to me. As the school year was drawing to an end, I decided I needed a fresh start, someplace where people didn't know me or my history, someplace where I wouldn't have all the constant reminders of that dark day.

"So, I decided it would be good for me to move far away. I began checking on-line for job openings, and that was when I came across the science position here at Jordan. After a couple phone interviews, I was hired. Since you guys are on a trimester system, I had to hurry and move as soon as the semester in Cleveland was over. So, that is my story of why I came to Jordan. I don't know why God took my wife so early in our marriage, but I do believe that God always has a reason for what He does, even when we don't understand it."

"Coach, we're so sorry about your wife. We had no idea," Buck said.

"It was not my intention to tell this story to get sympathy, but when you asked why I came to Jordan, I had to be honest with you. I just needed a new home where I could try to start over. I'm glad that I've been able to get to know all of you. Whether you know it or not, all of you have helped me get through a difficult time in my life, and I thank you for that."

"No, Coach, we thank you," Buck replied. "You have helped all of us change our lives. I think I can speak for all of us. Before you came to Jordan, we were all headed down the wrong path. Most of us didn't care about our grades. Our goal was to antagonize people, both students and teachers. Our mission was to disrupt things. That is how we defined success. We were probably in trouble more that we were out of trouble. As you've heard, many of us don't have great home environments, and that hasn't helped our situations. But, we are the ones that have ultimately made many bad choices in our lives. There was no motivation to change because no one cared about us – not until you came here. You've taught us and shown us that doing what is right is a good thing and that thinking more about others than ourselves is a godly thing. You've helped us get out of the pit we were in. So, we thank you!"

"Thank you for those kind words. I think we have all learned that God works in mysterious ways. Even in the little things, He has a plan."

The evening ended with lighter conversations, but they all left with a greater sense of God's direction in their lives and a deeper respect for one another.

Chapter 33

Over the past couple of weeks, Ben noticed that some of the School Board members had been around the school talking with various teachers and even some of the students. On one occasion he had actually seen the School Board President in the Principal's office. He hoped that his parting message to the Board members at the meeting had caused them to get more involved with the school rather than just be an administrative group.

As he entered his room on Monday morning, he was shocked to see Mr. Phelps, the Board President, already seated in the back of the room. Ben was surprised, to say the least, but he greeted him politely. "Good morning, Mr. Phelps. Are you visiting us this morning?"

"Yes, Mr. Harper. I decided that I needed to see for myself what goes on in your class. Any objections?"

"No," Ben said. "I'm glad that you are taking a greater interest in the welfare of the students." Ben wasn't trying to be sarcastic, but he really hoped Mr. Phelps' intentions were pure and objective. "If you will excuse me, Mr. Phelps, I need to get a few things ready for class."

This class was Ben's junior and senior science class, so Buck, Tommy, Sam, Zeke, and Rob were all going to show up in a few minutes. Ben knew that the presence of Mr. Phelps might generate some ill feelings with the boys because of what had taken place at the School Board meeting. He somehow needed to encourage them to have the right attitude. As he was writing some notes on the board for the students, it occurred to him that they all needed to love their enemy. They needed to show Mr. Phelps love, regardless of what he said or did. As Ben was finishing his notes, he casually moved to the right side of the chalk board, and in the upper right corner he wrote the number "6". He knew the boys would pick up on it. Rule #6 was "love your enemies".

The students all entered right on time. No one was ever late for Mr. Harper's class. As they were taking their seats, they all observed the man in a suit and tie sitting in the back of the room. Most of the students didn't recognize him, but the football players did. Ben immediately detected by the looks on their faces and their body language that negative feelings were starting to surface. After everyone had taken their seats, Ben introduced Mr. Phelps. "Class, I would like all of you to recognize Mr. Phelps, who is here to observe our class today. Mr. Phelps is President of the School Board. He has expressed interest in what we do in our class. Mr. Phelps, if you wouldn't mind, please join us in our circle. We like the circle format so that we can all see each other and interact with each other better."

Ben could tell that Mr. Phelps was not very comfortable with the idea of joining the group, but he did comply and moved his chair in line with the others. As it turned out, he was sitting right between Buck and Tommy. Ben could see their faces starting to get a bit red. Ben began, "Please direct your attention to the chalk board and notice what we will be covering today." Ben never began his class this way, but he wanted his players to see the number "6" in the upper corner of the board. Ben's players instantly saw it and knew the message he was conveying to them.

"OK," Ben said, "we'll get to our lesson in a minute, but as is our custom does anyone have a topic they would like to discuss this morning? Mr. Phelps, we usually spend just a few minutes at the beginning of each class period talking about any topic of concern that someone would like to raise for class discussion. We don't always solve a lot of problems, but it stimulates creativity and interaction. So, who would like to start it off?"

There was a long period of awkward silence, which was totally abnormal for this exercise. The kids always had something they wanted to discuss. Ben knew the silence was due to the presence of Mr. Phelps, who was a bit intimidating even when he didn't say anything.

Finally, the silence was broken when Mr. Phelps calmly said, "I have a topic for discussion, if that is OK?"

Ben responded, "Anyone is free to suggest a topic or raise a question, so please continue."

"My question is this – 'Is prayer effective?'" Again there was silence.

As Ben pondered the question, he realized that Mr. Phelps was trying to trap him. The school policy prevented any faculty or staff member from talking about God in school. If he responded to the question, he would have to choose his words carefully. Since this was meant to be a class discussion time, he said, "OK, class. Mr. Phelps has raised an excellent question." Ben wanted to be as positive as possible and not give the impression that Mr. Phelps had the upper hand or was in any way intimidating them with his question. "Would anyone like to offer any thoughts or comments?"

Sam politely raised his hand. Ben said, "Go ahead, Sam."

Our football team went to the hospital several weeks ago to visit Bobby Dyton. Mr. Harper prayed for him and he is now doing a lot better." Ben was glad Sam emphasized that he had prayed *in the hospital*. "I believe that God hears us when we pray and then acts according to His will."

A couple other students offered comments about their parents praying about things at home. Then Anne, who was usually very quiet, raised her hand. Though Anne was quiet, she commanded the respect of every student. When she spoke, they all listened.

"The answer to Mr. Phelps' question is both yes and no. In the Bible in the book of James it says 'the prayer of a righteous man is powerful and effective'[17]. Conversely, the verse implies that the prayer of an unrighteous man is not powerful or effective. So, the question is 'Who is righteous?' In the book of Romans, it says 'there is none righteous, not even one[18]. So, how can anyone be righteous? A little further in Romans it gives us the answer. It says 'We are made right in God's sight when we trust in Jesus to take away our sins[19]. So, only if we've trusted Jesus to take away our sins, are our prayers effective. If we've not trusted, then our prayers are not effective. In fact they are useless."

Everyone was a bit stunned by Anne's explanation, including Mr. Phelps. Ben knew that Anne had answered his question perfectly, and that she had certainly caught Mr. Phelps totally off guard.

Ben said, "Anne that was an excellent answer to a sometimes perplexing question. Thank you. Now it's time to get into our science lesson." During the class all of the students interacted well with each other and with Ben. Ben had a couple of hands-on items to help explain the lesson. Mr. Phelps observed that the students were very respectful of each other and even helped and encouraged each other. They all seemed eager to learn and were having fun doing it.

As class adjourned every one of the football players went over and shook Mr. Phelps hand and thanked him for coming to their class. Mr. Phelps had not expected that. In fact, his intentions in visiting the class were not entirely pure, and he was taken aback by the football players' kindness to him. He wasn't sure, however, whether their response was genuine or not.

---

[17] Ja. 5:16b – The prayer of a righteous person is powerful and effective. (NIV)

[18] Rom.3:10 – As it is written: "There is no one righteous, not even one;" (NIV)

[19] Rom. 3:22a – This righteousness is given through faith in Jesus Christ to all who believe. (NIV)

Mr. Phelps waited until all of the students had left the room before he got up to exit. Ben met him at the door. "Thank you for attending our class today. I wish all of the Board members would take this kind of interest in the students here at Jordan."

Mr. Phelps was feeling a little sheepish at this time knowing that his real reason for attending was not to show interest in the students, but to find something he could use against Ben. "It was extremely interesting, Mr. Harper. I've not seen this style of teaching before."

Ben wasn't sure if that was good or bad, but he tried to stay positive. "Well, Mr. Phelps, I invite you back any time. These are excellent kids! Far better than the credit most people give them."

"Thank you for the invitation, Mr. Harper. I might take you up on that some time."

Chapter 34

The week seemed to go by quickly. Ben had been busy preparing lessons, always trying to think of ways to maintain interest in the class.

The team worked hard preparing for their game Friday night. The hard work paid off as Jordan posted another victory, this time over Maytown by a score of 20 to 10. It was an away game and the Jordan crowd was the largest yet for an out of town event. Many of the townspeople were starting to come in addition to the students and their parents. It certainly encouraged the boys to have more fans cheering for them. Ben even noticed some of the Board members in the crowd, which he hoped was a good thing.

To Ben's surprise Mr. Phelps attended his science class again on Tuesday. Everyone was much more relaxed this time, including Mr. Phelps. For their pre-class discussion time one of the students asked if they could discuss ways to improve the appearance of the school. Compared to every other school in the area, Jordan was the most run down. One student suggested planting some new bushes and trees in front. Someone else suggested some fresh paint in the classrooms and hallways. Another mentioned a new sign out front. Buck then asked Mr. Phelps, "Is it possible for the school to do any of these things? I think it would really help student morale."

Mr. Phelps replied, "These are all great ideas, and I agree that they would probably help student morale, but the District just doesn't have the money to do them at this time."

Buck persisted, "But what if we got some kids to volunteer to help? A lot of us can paint or plant things, and we have a good shop class that could make a nice sign."

"I'm intrigued by your idea," Mr. Phelps said. "Let me discuss this with the other School Board members. If you all could provide a lot of the labor, it might not cost too much for the materials." They all thanked Mr. Phelps. Ben thought there might actually be a bit of bonding taking place; certainly not what he expected, but definitely a pleasant surprise.

The next football game was also an away game, against Capeton. Jordan's conference record was now 5 and 0, but Capeton was right behind them at 4 and 1. It would be another tough game as usual. The Booster Club had raised enough money from concession sales at the last two home games to pay for two student buses to go to the game. That hadn't been done for a long time, so it created a new sense of enthusiasm among the students. Everyone was amazed at how well the team was doing, especially given the circumstances. Jordan was the underdog in every game, but somehow they were finding ways to come out on top, and people were getting excited!

Both teams played good football. Ben didn't mix in any trick plays nor had he done so in the previous away game. The boys were playing well. They were playing as a team, and as a result they had been winning games. The game ended with Jordan on top 24 to 21. The Jordan crowd went wild as they were now tied for first place in the conference with Granton, their final opponent.

Before breakfast on Saturday morning, Ben retrieved the newspaper from his mailbox and as was his custom he read through it as he ate. He was particularly interested in what Mr. Baxter had written about Friday's game. There was only a short article giving the score and highlighting that Jordan was now 6 and 0 in the conference, tied with Granton. Ben had expected a little more, but he also realized that to get much of an article published by Saturday morning after a Friday night game had to be difficult.

On Sunday morning before church Ben once again grabbed the newspaper and turned to the sports section, hoping to find a little more on the team's success. As he opened the sports section, the headline in big bold letters read, 'DAVID VS GOLIATH – FRIDAY NIGHT'. Ben then proceeded to read the article.

174

"With their win last Friday night against Capeton, the Jordan Indians have somehow managed to compile a 6 and 0 record in the conference and 6 and 2 overall record. After losing the first two non-conference games, they now find themselves tied for first place with Granton. Their season scores show they have only won by a slim margin in all of their games.

Season Summary

L	Jordan	7	Applewood	34
L	Jordan	6	Gridley	7
W	Jordan	6	Franklin	3
W	Jordan	19	Danvers	14
W	Jordan	12	Alento	7
W	Jordan	18	Parksville	16
W	Jordan	20	Maytown	10
W	Jordan	24	Capeton	21

"Winning even one game would be considered remarkable given the fact that Jordan wasn't even supposed to have a team this year. That coupled with the fact that they only have twelve players total makes this string of victories a minor miracle. Heck, my daughter's dance class fields more than twelve members! It is hard to determine why this band of twelve is successful. They are certainly not your conventional team. Maybe their success is because they do this silent march around the field before each game, maybe it is because they have pre-game prayer on the field, maybe it is because they have twelve captains instead of one or two like normal teams, maybe it is because they don't have cheerleaders, or maybe it is just the blind luck of a coach that has never coached before (or hardly even played for that matter). Whatever reason you pick, you cannot deny that they have compiled an impressive win-loss record. In fact it has been over 20 years since a Jordan football team has achieved six consecutive wins in a season.

"But readers, I hate to lower the boom. This Friday night's game against the Granton Grizzlies will prove that luck doesn't always prevail. Just a few statistics on the Granton team will prove my point. They average 62 points per game. In fact they only have to score 14 points Friday night to break the all time State High School scoring record for a single season. The first two possessions should clinch that record! Their average win margin is 35 points per game. Their average weight of the front line on both offense and defense is 225 pounds. Compare that to Jordan at 175 pounds. Granton's biggest players are the left tackle at 6' 5" tall and weighing 260 pounds and the right tackle at 6' 3" tall and 240 pounds. Granton was the State champion last year and pollsters believe that no team in the State can come close to beating Granton this year.

"So I rest my case. My recommendation is to enjoy the team's success of the moment and don't be embarrassed when David meets Goliath on Friday night."

Well, Ben thought. That certainly doesn't paint a pretty picture for Jordan. He had heard a few things about Granton, but not all that was printed in this article. He actually hoped that the Granton team read this because Ben had learned that overconfidence on the part of the opponent could be a good thing.

Ben pondered the article most of the day, depressed at first but then several ideas popped into his head. He knew he would have to move fast since the game was less than a week away.

At school on Monday, it was hard to focus on school work because everyone was talking about football and the upcoming game (and the article in the Sunday paper). Ben had never seen so much excitement at Jordan High before.

Ben had one free period on Monday morning, so he took this time to meet with Mr. Fairfield, the band teacher. Ben had met Mr. Fairfield in the hallway a few times and they had always exchanged greetings. As Ben entered the band room, he was impressed with the neatness of the room and the pictures and posters hanging on the walls. It was easy to see that he loved music, and Ben suspected he was probably a perfectionist. "Mr. Fairfield, do you have a couple minutes?"

"Sure, come in Mr. Harper. What can I do for you?"

"I was wondering if you might have a trumpet player that would be willing to play the national anthem before the football game on Friday night. I thought the national anthem would be a nice touch for our last home game."

"I have several students that play the trumpet well, but Ricky Jones is a top notch player. He plays at a level far above the others. He is a very quiet person, though. He doesn't interact much with the other students. I'll have him in class after lunch. Would you like me to ask him if he would be interested?"

"Please do. He sounds perfect. If he is willing to do this, would you have him see me during study hall?"

"I'd be happy to, Mr. Harper. It would be good for Ricky to spread his wings a little. By the way, congratulations on your football season! You've done a great job with those kids, and you've certainly improved the morale around here."

"Thanks, Mr. Fairfield, I appreciate your kind words, but I've had some divine help."

"Hope you have a great game Friday night!"

"Thanks," Ben replied. "We'll need all the support we can get!"

During study hall, Ricky approached Mr. Harper. "Mr. Harper, I'm Ricky from band class. Mr. Fairfield said you would like me to play at the football game." Ben proceeded to tell Ricky about his idea for the game.

Before Ben left school at the end of the day on Monday, Miss Reed, the girls physical education teacher walked into his room. Ben was acquainted with Miss Reed. He had talked to her several times during lunch and at some of the after school activities during the past months. "Mr. Harper, I wanted to catch you before you left today."

"Please come in, Miss Reed," Ben said. "What brings you to my end of the building?"

"I've been approached by several junior and senior girls asking if they might be cheerleaders during your game Friday night. Obviously, they will not have had time to practice much, but most of them were cheerleaders last year. Last year was such a bad season, and everyone was really down. But now with your great season, everyone is very excited and the girls would really like to participate again, if that would be OK with you?"

"I'm not sure you need my approval, but I think that would be fantastic! Some crowd participation would be a huge motivation for the boys."

Suddenly, Ben had another idea, something the cheerleaders could help accomplish. He explained his idea to Miss Reed. "That's a great idea. I know the girls will be more than willing to do that!"

"Great," Ben said. "Thanks for all your help."

Ben was a few minutes late getting to practice after school. His conversation with Miss Reed had gotten him off schedule a bit, but it was worth the time. The boys were already doing their warm up exercises. They knew the routine and had started even though Ben wasn't there. They were good about taking the initiative. Ben admired them for that.

When Ben got on the field, he apologized for being late. He immediately sensed a negative spirit among the boys. Pete spoke up and said, "Did you read the article in the Sunday newspaper about Granton? It sounds like we don't have a chance. They've crushed every opponent they have faced."

Ben replied, "With God there is always a chance. Nothing is impossible with God[20]. Always remember that."

They all shook their heads, but Ben noticed that it was not with a lot of confidence. "OK, I know they are big and they score a lot of points and they are ranked No. 1, but that doesn't mean they aren't vulnerable. I've seen some great teams fall because they were overconfident. They are taking us for granted. I believe that will work in our favor. It is unlikely they have scouted us because until the last game or two we were not a conference contender. So, they don't know how we play. And furthermore, I have a few new plays that I want to work on this week. They are used to standard straight forward football. But we are going to think outside the box and mix things up for them, and maybe we can catch them off guard. Maybe we won't win, only God knows. But I don't want you to give up without doing your best. Who knows what might happen."

After talking some more as a team, everyone perked up and really became enthused about the game. They worked really hard in practice all week, and they had fun with the new plays Ben had created. These were certainly nothing they had ever seen before and hopefully Granton hadn't either.

On Thursday night after practice Ben told the boys, "The game starts at 7:00 tomorrow night. Instead of showing up at 6:00 like we normally do, I would like for all of you to be here at 5:15. We'll get dressed, do our warm up drills, and then meet in the Bus Garage. I want to go over a few things before the game. So, go

---

[20] Jer. 32:27 – "I am the Lord, the God of all mankind. Is anything too hard for me?" (NIV)

home, get a good night's rest, and let's see what tomorrow brings. Good practice tonight guys! I'll see you all at school."

Chapter 35

Ben had to confess that he didn't sleep very well Thursday night and he was having trouble staying on task in his science classes during the day on Friday. Not only was the game stealing most of his mental faculties, so was the thought that his job as teacher and coach at Jordan High might soon be over. The School Board had allowed him to continue until the end of the football season, and then they would make their decision. Ben had not heard anything one way or the other, not even a rumor, so anxiety was building. He had seen some of the Board members in the building a few times over the past few weeks, and Mr. Phelps had visited his class a couple times, but no one had made any revelation or comments that he had heard. He finally decided he needed to put the whole School Board thing out of his mind and stay focused on his classes. After all, his students deserved his full attention.

The day seemed to fly by. The final bell was ringing and kids were hurrying to leave school. He hoped the majority of them would be at the game, but he had no idea how many would show up, especially after the article in the Sunday newspaper.

Ben usually went home on Friday nights and ate a light meal before coming back for the game. But, not tonight, especially since he wanted the boys to be back early. He just needed some quiet time to think and to decide what to say to the boys to prepare them. He decided to go over to the Bus Garage, because he knew no one would be there at that time of day. He found that quiet meditation was good for the soul.

About 5:10 p.m. Ben headed back to the locker room to meet the boys. The boys all arrived promptly at 5:15 p.m. Everyone got dressed without saying much. The mood was much more somber than usual, sort of like waiting for the doctor to show up when you know the news will not be good. Ben hoped he could move them beyond what they were feeling and to find encouragement in what they had accomplished.

They walked onto the field about 5:30 p.m. There were only a handful of people around the field, mostly those setting up the concession stand. About 5:45 p.m., as they were doing their warm up drills, the Granton players' buses arrived. Typically most schools only had one player's bus, but because Granton had so many players they had to bring two buses. Ben could see the boys watching as player after player got off the buses and walked to the locker room. The line seemed endless. They overheard one player exclaim, "Look guys, they must be having a junior high scrimmage before the game." Then there was laughter. To add another layer of intimidation, no sooner had the players entered the locker room, when six student buses pulled into the parking lot filled with Granton students already cheering loudly for their team.

After about fifteen or twenty minutes, the Granton players entered the field and as they did Ben motioned for the boys to leave for the Bus Garage. As he did at every home game, Ben told the boys a story to help prepare them mentally for the game. Tonight was no exception.

Ben began, "Before our Franklin game, I told you the story about how the Israelites crossed the Jordan River. I also told you that before crossing they had to wander in the desert for 40 years because of disobedience. Twelve spies had gone into the land to check things out before everyone crossed the River. Ten spies came back with a bad report because the land was filled with giants, people that were bigger and stronger than the Israelites. They were fearful because they didn't think they could defeat them. God in essence said, 'Because you doubted me, you can spend the next 40 years in the desert thinking about it.' Tonight it looks like we are facing a team of giants. We've already crossed the Jordan River, so there is no turning back. We do not need to face this moment in fear, because I believe that God is on our side. Whether we win or lose on the scoreboard, the game belongs to the Lord. If we play to honor Him, then God will bring about the result that He desires.

"The Israelites were not experienced warriors. They didn't have high tech weapons or superior battle skills, but God led them through all kinds of victories. What they accomplished was unbelievable. Let's see what God has in store for us tonight.

"It has been our custom to walk around the field in silence before each game, just like the Israelites did at Jericho. But on the final day God told the Israelites to march around Jericho seven times and then to blow a loud trumpet. When they did, the walls of Jericho fell down and the Israelites captured the town. When we go back out, we are going to march around the field three times, rather than seven times. If we had more time, we would march seven times, but I think three times will suffice.

"This time Ricky from the band group is going to join us. On the third time around when I raise my hand, Ricky is going to blow his trumpet and I want all of you to yell as loud as you can. When the Israelites did this, God gave them victory. Now God didn't promise to give us victory tonight just because we march around the field and yell, but perhaps we can put a little fear in the minds of our opponent. Any questions?

"OK then, just one other thought. In the Bible in the Book of Psalms it says that God saw each one of us before we were even born, and He recorded every day of our lives before we even lived our first day[21]. That means that this game tonight has already been recorded in God's book. It is history! In God's eyes it has already happened. He knows who wins and who loses. We can't change history, but what we can do is to play our best to honor Him. I expect there will be a lot of trash talk and insults tonight, but remember our rules (ieb-sw-lepte). Don't give in to them. Keep your heads, just like you have done all season. Especially remember the last rule tonight – enjoy life, enjoy the game. Have fun,

---

[21] Ps. 139:15-16 – My frame was not hidden from you when I was made in the secret place, when I was woven together in the depths of the earth. Your eyes saw my unformed body; all the days ordained for me were written in your book before one of them came to be. (NIV)

183

regardless of what the outcome is. You guys are incredible. I wouldn't trade you for any team in the world. So let's see what God has recorded!"

As they left the Bus Garage, they were greeted by cheerleaders lining each side of their path. They hadn't had any cheerleaders all year, and they certainly hadn't expected any tonight. What a great surprise. As they jogged onto the track they also noticed that the Jordan stands were nearly full, and there was a long line of people still waiting to get into the field. It was definitely going to be standing room only. Ricky, the trumpet player, was waiting on the sidelines ready to join them. Bobby and his dad were also already on the sidelines waiting for the team.

It was a cool night with the temperature in the upper 50's. There was hardly any breeze and the sky was clear. It was a perfect night for a football game. Ben was glad to see so many fans. He hoped they were cheering for them and not just in the stands to watch a ranked team play. Time would tell.

Ben led the procession of his team around the track as was his custom. The Granton players had heard that Jordan did this ceremonial walk around the field before each game, but they had never seen them do it. They all took notice and poked a few verbal comments as they walked past, but the team remained resolute in their mission.

Mr. Baxter from the Jordan Chronicle was the announcer for the game. He was filling in for the regular announcer, who had become ill during the week. Ben wasn't sure this would be a positive change. He was just getting started when Ben and the boys began their march around the field.

"Well folks, welcome to Jordan High. Tonight the Jordan Indians take on the Granton Grizzlies. Be prepared to see history made tonight. Both teams have perfect conference records, 6 and 0, but Granton's overall season record is 8 and 0 compared with Jordan's at 6 and 2. Jordan has somehow managed to eke out victories in all of their conference games, but Granton has literally devastated all of their opponents. No team has even come close to the Grizzlies.

"Consider this folks; Granton only needs 14 points to beat the all time State scoring record for a single season. Expect that record to fall in the first quarter, if not in the first two possessions! Granton is ranked No. 1 in the State by the High School Athletic Association. They are last year's state champions and there is no one that is even a close contender for stopping them this year. They have two all state players on the team; halfback Dillon Brown No. 25, and tackle Mike Stomp No. 76. Brown not only broke the conference rushing record with an average of 180 yards per game this year, but if he gets at least 80 yards tonight he will break the State rushing record as well. Expect the old record to fall early in the game. Stomp is 6' 5" tall and weighs 260 pounds. He leads the conference with 15 tackles per game. The Grizzlies are a powerhouse football team. It is a rare privilege to have such a high class team on our field tonight.

"On the flip side of the coin please welcome your Jordan Indians. This is one of the most unconventional teams I have ever seen! They only have twelve players on the entire team, they don't have numbers on their jerseys so it is impossible to tell who is who, and they do this weird march around the field before each game, as you can see. Call it a good luck tactic, a rabbit's foot, or whatever, but I think it is simply strange. Folks, they are tied with the Grizzlies for first place in the conference, but it will take divine intervention for them to even stay close to the Grizzlies tonight. Welcome to 'David meets Goliath'."

Ben had requested that Miss Reed have the cheerleaders pass the word to all the Jordan spectators to be fairly quiet until they heard the trumpet blow, then to yell as loud as they could. Ben had no idea that there would be a standing room only crowd, so he didn't know if everyone would get the message. But as they continued to walk the three laps, the crowd became more and more quiet. When there was only one quarter of a lap to go, Ben raised his hand. Ricky then sounded a loud blast on his trumpet, the loudest blast Ben had ever heard, and the team began to yell. The crowd, too, understood the signal and began to yell. The roar of the crowd was deafening! It was like the noise was all contained in the football stadium and couldn't get out. The Granton team stopped their practice, one because they couldn't hear anything, and two, because they were spellbound by the magnitude of the noise. No team that Granton had ever encountered had fans that yelled like this. Even the Granton coaches were mesmerized by what they were witnessing. The yelling went on for nearly a minute before subsiding. Ben's team all looked at each other with smiles on their faces. This was so much different than the beginning of the season when no one even showed up to watch their games. The cheering of the crowd gave them renewed confidence.

As they finished their walk, Bobby was waiting for them and gave each of them a high five. He was thrilled to be on the field again with the team. He had his numbered pieces of cardboard all in sequence; ready for whatever number Coach might want.

Bobby had been getting stronger every day since his last episode. The doctors had been able to quickly get his medicine back on course and he was responding very well. He had been looking forward to this game all week. Fortunately, the weather was good so he had been cleared to attend.

The next event was the coin toss. As had become their tradition, all twelve Jordan players went to the center of the field to meet the referees and the Grizzlies' captains. The two all state players were the only captains, so the lineup was heavily skewed in favor of Jordan. The home team got to call the toss. It was Wes's turn and he called heads. The coin toss was tails, so Granton got to choose whether they would kick-off or receive. Since they wanted to make their presence known soon, they elected to receive. At the referees order, the players all shook hands. As the big Granton tackle shook their hands, he said, "You guys are going down tonight. You are history!"

That comment caught Buck by surprise. That is just what Coach had said, this game is already in God's history book. He knew it was meant to be a derogatory comment, but somehow he found comfort in knowing they were acting out what God already knew.

The boys all gathered in a circle around Ben as they knelt on one knee and prayed. "Lord, we commit this game to You tonight and we trust You to help us through it. Whether we win or lose may we play in such a way that You are glorified. And I further pray that others would see Your mighty hand at work in each of these boys. You have given us a great season and for that we are truly grateful. I thank you for each of these boys. Please keep them safe tonight. Please keep the other team safe as well. Help our eyes to be open so we can see the great things You do. Thank You, Lord. Amen." And they all echoed Ben's Amen.

Chapter 36

Then from the loud speaker came the message, "Ladies and gentlemen, please stand, remove your caps, and face the flag as Ricky Jones plays our national anthem. Both teams lined up along their sideline. Ben noticed, as did all the boys, that Granton's team had so many players that they filled the entire sideline from goal to goal. It was certainly impressive to see such a long line of players in full uniform, obviously new uniforms -- with the fancy striping and lack of stains. Many of the players had stars all over their helmets, rewards for good plays they had made. In contrast Jordan's twelve man team only filled a few yards on the sideline. Their pants were plain and darkened by stains from several seasons of play. Their jerseys were plain, no numbers or stripes, and their helmets had no stickers. Ben had stressed team play throughout the season and not individual performance. His plain Jane approach had brought them all closer together, but tonight would be the real test. Could they support and encourage one another as a team or would they be sidetracked by the power and glamour of their opponent.

Ricky stepped a few yards onto the field and turned toward the flag, which was flying at the south end of the track. The gentle breeze made the flag unfurl just as Ricky began. He played like he was at the Super Bowl. Every note was sharp, and crisp, and loud. It sent a ripple of goose bumps down Ben's back, and he was sure every other person in the stands had to feel the same way. There was complete silence as he played each note perfectly. Ben had never heard anyone play the national anthem any better than Ricky. It was a very moving experience, a perfect beginning to this conference finale.

It was now time for the game to begin. Ben didn't know how the boys felt, but he was more nervous than he could ever remember. The boys lined up for the kick-off and the referee blew his whistle to signal that play could begin.

Ben had Cody kick-off, since he had been the most consistent during the season. The ball bounced once on the twenty yard line and then was picked up by Granton's No. 20 running at full speed. He went right up the middle of the field. Everyone watched in amazement as the Granton blockers opened up the center of the field like a snow plow on a road grader. There was no stopping him.

As soon as No. 20 scored the touchdown, he spiked the football like he was some kind of super hero. The ball bounced on the grass and then rolled clear across the track, which surrounded the field. Will saw it go, so he jogged over and picked it up and handed it to the referee. The referee was impressed that this Jordan player had made this kind gesture, especially since they had just given up a touchdown.

As Will was retrieving the ball, No. 20 was ranting, "You guys are nothing! You need to go back and play with your junior high buddies. You're going down, just like all the other teams we've played."

Ben couldn't believe what just happened. Granton had scored with only twelve seconds running off the clock. His worst butterflies ever seemed to get even worse, if that were possible, and now hearing the verbal abuse from No. 20 made Ben feel really bad for his boys. Tonight was going to be a long night. He hoped they would be strong and maintain their composure. Granton kicked the extra point with ease and the score was suddenly 7 to 0.

"What did I tell you folks", the announcer blared over the loud speaker "this Granton team is a real powerhouse! Don't take your eyes off the field or you could miss something exciting."

Before Granton kicked off, Buck grouped the team and tried to encourage them. "OK guys, we got that first play behind us. We were all nervous. Now we just need to settle down and play our game. We have to work together and cover each other. These guys might be big, but that doesn't mean they're invincible. Let's go get them!"

As Granton kicked off, the ball sailed clear down to the five yard line where Rob caught it and started running toward the left side of the field. No. 15 from Granton was running full speed down the sideline in front of the Jordan fans. He was watching the ball more than he was watching where he was going. He obviously didn't see Tommy waiting to block him. Tommy lowered his shoulder and caught No. 15 at the waist line. Because he was running so fast, Tommy merely raised him straight up and he did a complete flip over Tommy's head. The crowd roared and Rob raced for the opening created by Tommy. He was able to return the ball to their 40 yard line before being tackled. Tommy looked back and saw No. 15 still lying on the field. He hurried back to make sure he was OK. He had the wind knocked out of him, but he was starting to breathe again. Tommy offered him his hand and helped him up. He seemed to crack a slight smile, as if to thank Tommy for the help.

Jordan only gained three yards in the next three plays and then had to punt. Though they weren't able to make a first down, they seemed to gain confidence after seeing Tommy's block. It gave them some assurance that they could play with the Grizzlies and not get run over by them.

The Grizzlies moved the ball up field, but only with short gains. It was obvious they were getting frustrated that they couldn't break away. Ultimately they had to settle for a field goal, which made the score 10 to 0. The first quarter ended with neither team making any other significant scoring threats.

Soon after the horn sounded ending the first quarter, the announcer gave his recap. "I'm really amazed that Jordan has been able to slow down this scoring machine. Expect that to change, though, as we move into the second quarter. Jordan has posed no real scoring threats -- and that is no real surprise against this team. All Stater, No. 25, Dillon Brown has 50 yards rushing in the first quarter, so he is well on his way to breaking the state rushing record."

Ben had only a couple minutes to talk to the boys while they were getting ready for the second quarter. "You guys are doing great! Keep up the good work. You can play with these guys. They

191

are not as good as they think they are." The boys were all panting from playing continually. Ben substituted his twelfth player on every play, but that didn't give anyone much of a break. At least the change in quarters gave them a couple minutes to rest.

The second quarter brought about more of the same. Jordan was giving up small gains, which allowed Granton to move slowly but consistently down the field. It looked like they would have another score in a matter of a few minutes. No. 25 was an elusive runner, and it was hard for Jordan to keep track of him.

Bobby had been fairly quiet along the sideline. Suddenly, he called out to Ben. "Coach, I think I've figured it out."

"What do you mean, Bobby?"

"No. 25 -- I've been watching him carefully, and if he is going to carry the ball he always takes a quick look at where he is going to run just before the ball is snapped."

"You're kidding!"

"No, every time. Watch him on this play."

Ben focused on No. 25 as their team lined up on the ball. He took a quick look at the right tackle position. It was third down with 5 yards to go. Ben quickly called time out. He started onto the field and then motioned for Bobby to join him. Bobby was thrilled and ran out alongside Ben. The referee stopped them. "What are you doing, coach? You can't take a kid onto the field."

"He's my assistant. What is wrong with that? Granton has four assistant coaches, why can't I have one?"

"Alright. He is only a kid. What does he know?"

Ben had a bit of a smirk on his face as he and Bobby hurried to the huddle. "Coach, what's up?" Buck asked.

"Bobby figured out No., 25's weakness. Tell them Bobby."

"Me?"

"Yeah, you're my assistant!"

Bobby began with great excitement. "I've been watching No. 25 for several plays. If he is going to get the ball, he always looks in the direction he's going to run right before they snap the ball. If he's not going to get the ball, then he either looks down or straight ahead."

Ben chimed in, "That means we know if he is going to get the ball, and we know where he is going to run. They hardly ever use him as a pass receiver, so we can hone our defense by keying off him. Zeke, since you are playing middle line backer right now, you will have the best vantage point to see where No. 25 looks. When you see him, merely call out the name of our player that he will be running towards. Everyone needs to help out to stop him. If he isn't getting the ball, then call out 'N' for no. If that's the case, it probably means they are going to pass. Any questions?"

"Yeah," Buck said, "how did you figure that out, Super Spy?" as he looked at Bobby. Bobby had a big grin on his face as he thought about 'Super Spy'.

The next play No. 25 looked toward the right end where Sam was playing. Zeke quickly yelled "Sam", so they all figured it was going to be an end run in Sam's direction. They flooded the right side of the field and tackled No. 25 for no gain.

The Grizzlies tried a field goal from 35 yards, but it was wide to the right, so the score remained 10 to 0. Jordan held their own for the rest of the quarter, but they weren't able to get even close to scoring.

Chapter 37

Half time was a welcome break for the boys. They went to the Bus Garage where they could rest and talk about what they needed to do for the second half. The cheerleaders had really fired up the Jordan fans, which had helped the boys tremendously. Ben allowed Bobby to join them in the Bus Garage. That was a totally new experience for him. He sat quietly, taking in everything. He was really impressed with Coach Harper. He never got angry with any of the guys. He was always encouraging them, no matter what happened. Bobby liked that. Ben had made him feel good, too, by making him his assistant.

"I think the second half we are going to start using some of the plays we've worked on in practice. You guys are doing great on defense, but we have to find a way to score. Buck and Pete, you're blocking the big guys. If they are coming in standing up, block them low to take them down. That may give us time to get our runners past them. For now take a few more minutes to rest before we go back out."

They all welcomed the rest. They were exhausted, but they knew they had a long second half to go. Finally, it was time to go back onto the field. As they walked out, they received a standing ovation and a roaring welcome from the Jordan crowd. This whole crowd thing was foreign to them. It certainly activated the adrenaline.

The kick-off went to Wes, who made a running catch and started through a hole on the right side. Two or three of his teammates were ahead of him ready to block. He plowed his way to the 35 yard line before being stopped. Ben knew they were going to have to take more chances, if they had any hope of scoring. To mix things up he called for a flair pass to Will on the right side. It was a quick pass and gained them five yards. Then on a quick count they ran Corky up the middle and gained three more yards. It was third down with two yards to go. This time he had everyone pull to the right to block for an end run, except Zeke was to fake a hand off to Corky and run a keeper around the left end. Zeke had become a pro at hiding the ball on his hip. His fake handoff was perfect and no one suspected he had the ball. As the entire defense moved in Corky's direction, Zeke began running in the opposite direction. He made it across the fifty yard line before the defensive safety caught him. It was a gain of almost 20 yards, the longest of the evening for Jordan. The Granton coach was furious. Everyone could hear him screaming even above the noise of the crowd.

Next Ben had the boys run a scramble play, where all the team members moved to a different position before the ball was snapped. It looked like random chaos, but when it was coupled with a quick snap, Granton was caught in total confusion. During the play Cody moved from right guard to quarterback. He threw a perfect strike to Rob who was running a deep out pattern. It was another gain of 15 yards. It was now first and ten on the 22 yard line.

Ben had them run the "peanut shuffle", a new play they'd worked on in practice. The play required a full backfield – two halfbacks and a fullback, except the two halfbacks faced backwards (their backs to the line of scrimmage). Zeke would take the ball from the center and hand it to one of the halfbacks or keep it himself. The three of them would all run in different directions, pretending to conceal the football. It was like putting a peanut under one of three cups and then moving them all around to confuse the person guessing. The fullback was to block any opposing player that may have gotten through the line. All the linemen tried to block low and knock their opponents down. On the snap Zeke quickly moved between the halfbacks who were standing close together. No one could see who ended up with the ball. They all ran in different directions. The defense had no idea who to chase. Corky actually ended up with the ball and was able to run for ten more yards. It was now first and ten on the 12 yard line.

The next play they ran in stealth mode. With this play Zeke didn't make any call. He didn't even say "down" to get the team in position. They all walked to the line silently, held their position without moving to prevent having an illegal procedure call, then they would snap the ball on whatever delay count Zeke had called in the huddle. The count started as soon as the center touched the ball. The boys all had to count silently "1001, 1002," etc. to make sure they were in unison and didn't jump before the ball was hiked. They had practiced this many times and had it down to perfection.

Zeke called for the snap as soon as the center touched the ball – no delay. Since the usual practice for any quarterback was to yell out the count, Granton was totally unprepared for a silent snap. Zeke handed off the ball to Corky for another five yard gain. They lined up again in the same fashion with no one saying a word, but this time Zeke had called for a two count delay. As soon as the center touched the football, No. 76, Granton's big tackle, jumped off sides. He was expecting another quick snap. That resulted in a five yard penalty.

Now it was first and goal on the two yard line. This time they ran their scramble play again with Tommy running a quarterback sneak. He barely made it through the front line, but it was far enough for a touchdown. The crowd went wild. The entire Jordan team was jumping for joy. Bobby was so excited he could barely contain himself. The Grizzlies on the other hand were yelling at each other and pointing fingers at who missed the tackle. Their coach was pacing the sideline kicking the dirt and yelling obscenities at any player in his path.

The extra point attempt failed, so the score was now 10 to 6. That score seemed to super energize Jordan. "I can't believe it," the announcer proclaimed. "That was an incredible series of plays by this 'never say die' team. Who would have thought they could ever stay this close to Granton. These guys have a lot of heart, but much of the game still remains."

The rest of the third quarter was back and forth with no major gains by either team. Keying off No. 25 proved to be a huge benefit for Jordan. They were able to stop him almost every time. He was getting more and more frustrated, as was the whole team. Granton was beginning to realize that their image would be severely tarnished if they couldn't put together a better game than this, especially against this band of nobodies.

The first few minutes of the fourth quarter began the same. The Grizzlies had the ball. No. 25 was running the ball but tripped over his own player and fell hard to the ground. The entire team was so angry as they returned to their huddle that they didn't even realize No. 25 was slow in getting up. Buck and Tommy saw him on the ground and realized that he had twisted his ankle. So they helped him up and carried him over to the Granton sideline. When they got him to a bench, Buck said with a sincere heart, "I hope you are OK. We didn't want anyone to get hurt tonight. I hope you can make it back into the game."

Embarrassed because of his previous attitude, No. 25 sheepishly said, "Thank you for helping me." Everyone on the Granton sideline was astonished at what they had just witnessed. They had ridiculed Jordan all night long, and now their opponent was repaying evil with good.

With three minutes to go in the game Jordan was forced to punt. Granton caught the ball on the five yard line, but was tackled quickly by Jordan. Granton ran the ball on the first play, but only made a couple yards. It appeared that all Granton had to do was continue making short gains on the ground, and they could run out the clock. But embarrassed by the score, Granton decided to put the game out of reach by throwing a long pass on second down.

Cody was on the runner going deep, but the opponent was about five inches taller than Cody. The pass soared about 40 yards in the air and the receiver was in full stride. If the pass was anywhere close, the runner would be able to reach above Cody and grab the ball. If that happened, it would become an easy score. Ben was holding his breath as he watched the ball. Pete was running over from the center of the field to help out, but it didn't appear that he would get there in time. As the ball started its downward trajectory, Ben noticed that it was slightly under thrown, but potentially still in reach of the runner.

Just as the ball was within reach of the opponent's hands, Cody leaped with all his might and caught the nose of the ball with one finger. It was just enough to deflect the ball out of reach of the receiver. Cody tumbled to the ground. What he didn't know was that he had deflected the ball just enough for Pete to make an interception. Everyone in the stands was on their feet yelling for Pete to go. He managed to pick up a couple good blocks from Wes and Russ before he was tackled at the 20 yard line. The clock was now stopped with only two minutes remaining.

Ben had Bobby hold up the No. 9 card, "I will be a team player." Granton was sure this was some kind of trick play, so they anticipated something weird. But Jordan ran a normal play further confusing the Grizzlies. They gained five yards. Ben had them mix things up with their scramble plays and stealth mode. They were able to get down to the three yard line, but Granton was holding strong. They were a good team, and they weren't giving up. There was only five seconds left on the clock, time for one more play. Ben quickly called time out.

Ben and Bobby jogged out to the huddle with the boys. As soon as they arrived, Buck said, "Coach, what are we going to do? They are stopping us every time."

Ben thought for a moment, "As I see it, we have three options: 1) we try to go around them, 2) we try and go through them, or 3) we try and go over them." Suddenly a light came on in Ben's mind. "How did David defeat Goliath?"

Someone answered, "With a sling shot."

"That's right. That's exactly what we are going to do." Ben had another time out to use, so he called it to have more time to explain his plan. Jimmy was the smallest player on the team at only 125 pounds. "Jimmy, you like to do tumbling, right? I've seen you guys mess around on the field during practice, and you're pretty good."

"Yeah, Coach. I took lessons a few years ago, but I still like doing it."

"Good, so here is what we are going to do. I want everyone to take their normal positions. When Zeke calls out 'S' for scramble, I want you to move to new positions, but not like we normally do. Zeke, you move from quarterback to the left end position. Rob, you move from halfback to the right end. Pete, you move from fullback to center. Buck and Sam, you are our two biggest guys. I want you to move to the halfback positions. And Jimmy, you're going to be our quarterback. When the ball is hiked, I want all the pass receivers to run down and out patterns to draw the line backers away from the center of the field. If we put our smallest player as quarterback and our two biggest guys as halfbacks, hopefully they will think we are going to pass, especially since we've not been able to run well on the last few plays. You linemen, especially in the center need to knock your opponents down, if at all possible.

"Hike the ball straight to Jimmy, who will be set up in a shotgun formation. Jimmy, you make a quick fake like you are going to pass. Buck and Sam, you turn and face each other and lock hands. Jimmy is then going to run up on your hands while you sling shot him over the goal line. The timing is critical and I realize we have never practiced this, but I know you guys can do it. Our time is about up. Does anyone have any questions?"

"Yeah, Coach, has this ever been done before?" Sam inquired.

"Well, not to my knowledge, but there is a first time for everything! OK, guys, now is the time."

Ben and Bobby hustled off the field. Ben was suddenly flooded with all kinds of emotions. This would be the last play of the game, and possibly the last play of the season for his team. It could well be the last game of his coaching career, and possibly the end of his teaching career at Jordan High, depending on how the

School Board decided to act. But regardless of how things turned out, it had been an amazing journey. A few tears trickled down his cheek as he reached the sideline and turned to face his team.

The fans on both sides of the field were on their feet, waiting anxiously for this last play. Finally the referee signaled for play to resume. The boys lined up like normal, then Zeke yelled out 'S', and they all scrambled to their new positions. Jimmy took over as quarterback. He yelled out "Down, hike."

The snap was flawless, and Jimmy faked a pass to the right side. Granton's linebackers took the bait and followed Jordan's receivers as they ran their outside pass patterns. That left the center of the field open. Jimmy then gripped the ball tight with both hands. From that moment on, the play for Ben seemed to move in super slow motion. Granton's big line men were rushing hard, but Jordan's guys blocked them low and several of them tumbled to the ground just as Jimmy sprang onto the locked hands of Buck and Sam. Buck and Sam heaved with all their strength. The timing was perfect and they sent Jimmy airborne over the Granton linemen and into the end zone. Jimmy clutched the ball tightly to avoid a fumble. For a moment after hitting the ground, he wasn't sure what happened, and neither did anyone else on the Jordan team. Then they heard the referee's whistle blow and the call "touchdown!" Time had expired and Jordan had defeated the Grizzlies 12 to 10.

The boys were ecstatic, jumping up and down, hugging each other. Bobby was jumping up and down with Ben on the sideline. Ben grabbed him off the ground and gave him a big hug. The Jordan crowd went wild and started flooding the field.

The announcer proclaimed with a choked up voice, "I can't believe what just happened! This little band of twelve Jordan players has just defeated the No. 1 team in the State of Kansas. In my wildest dreams, I never thought this was even remotely possible." Obviously, Granton didn't think so either as they hung their heads and retreated to the sideline. Buck led the way and every member of the Jordan team went to the Granton sideline and shook the hand of every player and every coach -- not to rub salt into their wound, but to demonstrate good sportsmanship. Not all of the Granton players returned a friendly handshake, but No. 25 realized he wasn't half the player as these boys from Jordan. He congratulated them on their victory and apologized for the words he'd spoken earlier in the game.

The boys then returned to the center of the field and enjoyed time with their fans. Buck and Tommy lifted Bobby up on their shoulders and carried him around as their hero in victory. Bobby was all smiles. You couldn't tell he had been deathly ill just a few weeks ago. The announcer finished his comments by concluding, "This has to be one of the greatest games in the history of this conference, if not one of the greatest games in the history of the State. Tonight, David defeated Goliath!"

In the Sunday paper, Mr. Baxter had a big article on the football game. He titled it "THE GIANT GOES DOWN" and it featured a picture of Jimmy in mid air as he crossed the goal line. The article had a much different tone than the previous one. He had high praise for the boys and their accomplishments. After all the boys had been through, Ben was glad to see they were getting a little more respect.

That game was the talk of the town and at school all week. Ben thought it was funny how one game could change the attitude of so many people. It was like everyone had received a shot of penicillin. Their old wounds were no longer critical. They now had a more positive outlook all because twelve boys decided to work hard and work together. In the Bible, Joshua had defeated Jericho. David had defeated Goliath. Now Jordan had defeated Granton. What was next for the town of Jordan? Only God knew the answer to that question. But whatever it was, Ben knew that God had it already figured out.

Chapter 38

Jordan won their first two state tournament games before falling in a close game to the eventual State championship team. They played their best in every game, and they ended up as one of the top eight teams in the State. Not bad given where they had started.

Now that the season was over, the fear of School Board action had returned to Ben's mind. He hadn't heard anything pro or con about his continuation. The anxiety was starting to build.

The Booster Club planned a big celebration for the team on Friday night. It was open to the public, so to handle the anticipated crowd they made arrangements to hold the event at the National Guard Armory. That facility was much larger than the school gymnasium. Ben and all the team members received a special invitation, and Ben was asked to say a few words about their season.

Ben wasn't sure what to expect, so he arrived a few minutes early. Mrs. Brown, head of the Booster Club, explained the sequence of events. "We want you and the team to sit on the left side of the stage, and on the right side we will have Mr. Phelps, the School Board President, Mr. Reed, the Principal, and Mr. Baxter from the newspaper. As we indicated before, we'd like you to speak for a few minutes, if you don't mind. Then each of the other gentlemen will follow with some additional words. We will plan to start promptly at 7:00 p.m. Any questions?"

"Yes, I have one. Would it be OK if Bobby also joined the boys up on the stage? Obviously, he is not a player, but he was a major factor in the success of the team."

"If you don't think the players would be offended, that is fine with me."

"I'm sure they would be pleased to have him join them."

Ben greeted all the boys as they came in and told them where to sit. Ben also saw Bobby and his parents enter. He quickly told Bobby that he could sit with the team. Bobby couldn't believe they would let him do that. Ben noticed that Bobby's hair had been growing back and he had gained some weight. He looked so much better than when Ben and the team saw him the first time in the hospital. It was truly a miracle that Bobby had returned to good health. Truly a miracle, Ben thought, but then miracles are God's specialty! Bobby was all smiles as he took his seat with them.

Ben had a queasy feeling about the lineup of speakers that Mrs. Brown had indicated. None of them had been on his top ten list of supporters! And there was still the question of his ongoing employment. He hadn't changed any of his routines since the School Board meeting several weeks ago. Would they make an announcement tonight in front of all these people? If so, that would be very awkward, Ben thought.

Mrs. Brown approached the microphone promptly at 7:00 p.m. and requested that everyone be seated. The room was packed full of people – students, teachers, parents, and many others from around town. "Ladies and gentlemen, the Booster Club has organized this event tonight to give special recognition to our high school football team for their stellar season. It has been many years; in fact I can't remember how long, since we've had this privilege to honor a local team. But tonight we've tried to bring everyone together for this special celebration. We have Coach Harper and his team sitting up here. Coach Harper has agreed to make a few comments about the season. Then we will also hear some remarks from Mr. Reed our high school Principal, Mr. Baxter the sports editor from the Jordan Chronicle and also the game announcer for the last conference game, and finally from Mr. Phelps the School Board President. So, to begin the evening we would like Coach Harper to come and speak. Coach Harper, I'll turn the program over to you."

Ben stood up and slowly approached the microphone, not sure he was ready for this. "Public speaking has never been one of my strong points, especially in crowds this size, so please bear with me. Thank you for having this event tonight. We are honored by your kindness and support. When I came to Jordan High last spring, I came as a science teacher. I love teaching science to young people. That is my passion. Coaching football was never on my radar screen. But one day last summer some of the boys in my science class brought up how much they wanted to play football, but as you know the football program had been cancelled following the end of last season. They asked if I would talk to Mr. Reed to see if he might allow the football program to continue. Mr. Reed agreed, but with the understanding that there was no budget for any football expenses. After much thought and prayer, I agreed to be the coach, not because I had any great coaching experience, but because I viewed it as an opportunity to teach the boys some valuable lessons about life.

"It is my belief that being able to participate in sports is a privilege, and that those participating should strive for higher standards in their lives. God has given each of us different abilities. If we use our individual abilities in conjunction with others, great things can be accomplished. I believe that being a team member means always viewing your teammate as more important than yourself. Fortunately, not many of you were at our first game against Applewood. It was not pretty! We had twelve players, but we did not have a team. Everyone was playing for their own benefit and not for the benefit of the team. Gaining personal glory was the goal that night. Unfortunately, I think that is the motivation for many sports players today. I then realized we needed to make a lot of changes, if we were going to be a team.

"The weekend after that game a good friend of mine brought to my attention a young football enthusiast that was suffering from leukemia. He was at the hospital here in Jordan. She suggested that he might benefit from a visit from our football players. I did not know this young boy at the time, but I called the hospital and talked to his parents to make sure they were OK with a visit. That Monday night I took the boys to the hospital to meet seven year old Bobby Dyton. We weren't sure what to expect when we entered his room, but we soon came to love this little guy that was struggling for his life. Despite his difficult situation, he had a smile that wouldn't quit. We had a great visit that night and two things happened; 1) these boys realized that viewing other people as more important than themselves is better than any trophy that might sit on their shelf, and 2) Bobby became their biggest fan. We entered Bobby's room that night to encourage him. We left his room encouraged by him. We entered Bobby's room as twelve players. We left Bobby's room as one team. That night Bobby became our inspiration!

"Bobby, would you come up here?" Bobby wasn't sure what to do, but he got up slowly and with a big smile on his face, he walked over to Ben. Ben put his hand on Bobby's shoulder as the two of them stood together before the crowd. "Bobby is my assistant coach!" There were chuckles in the crowd, but Ben continued. "You probably aren't aware of this, but Bobby is a big reason for our win over Granton. On his own he figured out a major weakness in the Granton offense. I think everyone on the team would agree that if Bobby had not figured that out, we would not be here tonight."

Bobby looked up at Ben and asked if he could talk. Ben appeared a bit puzzled, but he pulled up a chair for Bobby to stand on. "My assistant coach would like to say a few words."

"I just want to say that Coach Harper didn't tell you the whole story. When the team came to my hospital room that night, the doctors didn't think I would live much longer. They didn't exactly tell me that, but I knew. I was getting weaker every day. I really needed a bone marrow transplant, but nobody could be found that was a match. After these guys left my room, they all decided to be tested to see if their bone marrow might be similar to mine, including Coach. God performed a miracle because one of these guys was a match for me, and he was willing to give his bone marrow to help me. I don't know who it was, but they all volunteered. If the team hadn't done that for me, I'm sure I would not be here tonight either. Thank you guys for saving me!"

The audience all stood and gave little Bobby a standing ovation. It was a moment to be treasured. Bobby's parents were seated in the front row. They both had tears of joy streaming down their faces.

When the clapping stopped, Ben resumed. "I think you can all see that this is one tough little kid, and I predict that he will be a great football coach someday. Thank you, Bobby, for your help this season."

With that Bobby went back to his seat with the players, waving to the crowd. "My final comment is this: It has been a great privilege for me to coach these boys this season. I am extremely proud of each one of them. They have shown courage and determination in so many areas, not just on Friday nights. I hope that their conduct throughout this season has inspired all of you to live to a higher standard and to honor God in all that you do. They are certainly an inspiration to me. Thank you."

Before Ben could resume his seat, Mrs. Brown approached the microphone and spoke, "Coach Harper, I know this wasn't on the agenda tonight, but would you and your team be willing to answer a few questions from the crowd? I suspect people may have a few things that they would like to ask."

"Well, I guess so – as long as the questions aren't too hard!"

"OK, then, does anyone have a question they'd like to ask Coach Harper or his team?"

One lady raised her hand. Ben recognized her as a teacher he'd seen at one of the conferences he had attended. "Coach Harper, some of us heard that before coming to Jordan you had a good teaching position at a really nice school in Cleveland, Ohio. What prompted you to leave all of that and come way out here?"

Wow, Ben had to swallow hard on that question. He assumed the questions would be football related, not personal. He had told his story to Ruth when he first moved into her rental house, and he had told the boys the night of their cookout, but he hadn't told anyone else. It was a painful story to tell, even more so in front of a big crowd. But as Ben looked over at his players, he knew he had to be a man of integrity, his No. 1 Rule, and not sidestep the issue, even though it would be difficult.

Ben hesitated for a few seconds and prayed silently for strength. Then he slowly began. "It is true that I had a good teaching job in a well-to-do high school in Cleveland as a science teacher. I loved my job and I loved the kids I was teaching. My wife, Amy, was a grade school teacher (he had to pause for a few moments to regain his composure) at a nearby school in Cleveland. We were married right out of college, and we were fortunate to both find jobs in the same school district. One morning on her way to school an elderly gentleman had a heart attack and ran a red light. He hit my wife's car broadside (he hesitated again trying to fight back the tears), and she was killed instantly. I apologize, as you can tell I still struggle with this. I continued to teach through the end of the school year, but I decided a couple months before the end of school to look for a different job. I was having trouble coping with the memories. I just wanted to get away and start over. So, I looked on the internet and found that Jordan had an opening. I was interviewed over the phone by Mr. Reed and some of the School Board members, and it came about that they were willing to hire me. Since your school is on a trimester system, I had to hurry and pack to get here in time for your spring session. Anyway, that is my story. It was hard letting go of my wife, but I know that God had a reason for taking her home to heaven. I believe that God directs our steps. He had a reason for bringing me here."

"Thank you, Mr. Harper. I can tell that was not an easy story to share. We appreciate your honesty. Does someone else have a question?" as Mrs. Brown motioned to the audience.

A middle aged man raised his hand. "Coach Harper, I was able to attend several of your final games, and I was very intrigued by some of the unique things that you did. I commend you for your creativity. I was wondering if you could share your play-calling technique, when you occasionally held up the numbered cards."

"That is an interesting question, because the numbered cards didn't actually have anything to do with calling plays. It was merely a way for me to remind the boys of a rule they needed to apply. I realize that in several games it totally confused our opponents, but it really wasn't designed to do that."

The man replied, "Now I'm even more intrigued. What are the rules you are talking about?"

"Well, as we started the football season I asked all of the boys to commit to following ten rules. These aren't just rules that apply to football, but rules that apply to all of life. Football just happens to provide an excellent training ground. My goal was to teach them how to live in a way that honors God now and also in the future. Honoring God means we have to live by a higher standard than what the world lives by. I think I'll have the boys tell you what the rules are. They have learned them well. Wes, why don't you start and then each of you recite one."

"Rule #1 – I will be a man of integrity."

"Rule #2 – I will encourage others."

"Rule #3 – I will bear others burdens."

"Rule #4 – I will not speak unwholesome words."

"Rule #5 – I will work hard."

"Rule #6 – I will love my enemies."

"Rule #7 – I will endure insults."

"Rule #8 – I will not pollute my body."

"Rule #9 – I will be a team player."

"Rule #10 – I will enjoy life."

"So, you can see these rules had nothing to do with calling plays, even though our opponents may have thought so! My hope was that if the boys could learn these rules and apply them in a football setting, then they would be well prepared for whatever circumstances that might come their way in life. I'm certainly not intelligent enough to come up with these rules on my own. They all come from the Bible. God gave us these rules so that by obeying them we would bring honor to Him, which is our ultimate goal in life."

Another lady raised her hand with a question, "Coach Harper, before football began my son was getting D's in all of his classes. Now he has a C+ average. How did you help him to improve his grades so much?"

"Our Rule #5 says that 'I will work hard'. That means not just on the football field, but in school, at home, at a job – whatever the task is. I believe that most students with a little help and encouragement can do better than they are doing. For the most part the boys helped each other – Rule #4. After almost every practice we would spend a half hour or so doing homework. If someone was having trouble, then one of his teammates that understood it better would help him. Most of these boys are good in at least one subject, so that gives them an opportunity to help someone that isn't. I also told them before football started that they were required to maintain at least a 'C' average in order to play. I know the school policy only requires a 'D' average, but I wanted these boys to realize that they could do better than that, and hopefully by doing so, set an example for others in school. When we started studying together, it really became a big benefit on the field also."

"Coach Harper, can you explain why you had the team wear jerseys with no numbers? It was almost impossible to tell who was who during the games."

Ben thought for a minute before he answered. "I believe that we must be very careful when we consider the attitude of pride. Being proud is dangerous and can easily lead to downfall[22], whether it is on the football field or in day to day life. We like to be proud because we think it puts us above others. If someone on the team thinks he is better than someone else, then we don't play together very well. The reason we have jerseys without numbers is so that people would have a hard time keeping statistics on each player. I want the boys to play as a team, not as individuals. If we score a touchdown, it is a touchdown by the whole team, because it took everyone to make it happen. Everyone should get the credit, not just one person. That is the same reason why we have twelve captains, because I believe they are all of equal importance."

Mrs. Brown stood up from her chair and once again approached the microphone. "We have time for one more question, if someone has one."

Someone in the back of the room raised his hand. "Coach, I don't know how you did it, but in my opinion you've worked a miracle in what you've accomplished with this team this year, not just on the football field, but with their attitudes, with their grades, and showing them how to work together. Their example has even improved my attitude. I just want to know if you're going to coach again next season."

Ben wasn't sure how to answer that question, since he hadn't received any indication from the School Board. "I would love to continue what we have started. I love these guys and I love all my students, but I'm not sure that decision is up to me. Thank you again for all your support. There are many people outside this team that had a role in making all this happen. We appreciate all of you."

---

[22] Pr. 16:18 – Pride goes before destruction, a haughty spirit before a fall. (NIV)

With that Ben sat down with his team, as the crowd rose to give him a standing ovation. Ben was humbled by their expression of love. He and his team stood and waived their hands in appreciation.

Mrs. Brown then announced," Now welcome our high school Principal, Mr. Reed." The crowd clapped softly as Mr. Reed approached the microphone. Ben wasn't sure if the lack of enthusiastic applause was due to Mr. Reed's reputation or due to the fact that most people didn't really know him.

"It was just about one year ago, Mr. Krank, our previous science teacher, told me he was planning to retire at the end of the school year. I sort of filed that in the back of my mind and with the holidays and everything associated with the New Year. I didn't begin thinking about finding a new science teacher until late February. And after further procrastination, it was late March when I finally decided I needed to take some action. We posted a listing with the State, but we really didn't receive any legitimate applicants. So, as a last resort I posted the job opening on the internet. To my surprise I only had one person respond, and that was Mr. Harper. And as Mr. Harper explained, we corresponded a few times. I only had two weeks to get a teacher on staff, so more out of desperation than thorough research, we made Mr. Harper an offer and well -- the rest is history.

"I have to confess that I have not been overly friendly to Mr. Harper. The stress of running a school, making sure that we get kids from one grade to the next so that we are eligible for State aid, trying to keep our finances in the black -- well, my focus had become severely skewed from what it should have been. I soon learned that Mr. Harper is not your typical teacher. He does things differently than what we've always done around here, and honestly, that rubbed me the wrong way. I had enough problems to handle without getting him in line with our program. He requested to do some unique things and because I didn't want to create another conflict, I gave him permission to proceed. I can honestly say that I have learned a valuable lesson from Mr. Harper, and that is that

212

people are more important than the process. You see, I had lost my focus on the needs of the students and was more concerned about merely pushing them from one grade to the next. I've been watching Mr. Harper's students. Almost every student has a higher science grade now than when he or she started the trimester. I know that is due to his personal concern for each student, and his ability to motivate them to work hard. This football team is a prime example of Mr. Harper's ability to do what no one thought was possible. Mr. Harper, please accept my apology for my cold shoulder, and thank you for showing me that the students are the most important thing.

"And to you boys on the team, I congratulate all of you for an unbelievable season. All of us at Jordan High are very proud of you. You have changed the attitude of our whole school. You are a tremendous example for all of us. Thank you."

The crowd clapped with tremendous enthusiasm as Mr. Reed concluded his remarks. It was obvious that the crowd was moved by Mr. Reed's change of heart.

Mrs. Brown then introduced the next speaker. "Now ladies and gentlemen, boys and girls, we are privileged to have Mr. George Baxter address us tonight. He is the sports editor for the Jordan Chronicle, and our game announcer for the last home game. As some of you know, Mr. Baxter was selected as a first team all state player from Jordan High twenty-five years ago. He is obviously an avid sports fan and has been employed by the Chronicle since completion of his college football career. Please welcome Mr. Baxter."

Ben was unaware of Mr. Baxter's football background. Perhaps that explained some of his negative comments about the team that seemed to dominate his written articles and his play by play calls during the game. Ben's technique was probably totally different than what he knew, and perhaps he was a bit jealous of the team's success, especially since they couldn't boast any all state players.

"I have been asked to make a presentation tonight, but before I do that there is one other thing I must do. From the bottom of my heart I want to apologize to Coach Harper and this team for all the negative things I have said about them over the season. I had a very judgmental attitude and always assumed the worst. I was wrong. Please forgive me.

"In all my years of playing and watching sports I have never seen a group of players function as a team better than these guys. They have raised the bar. They have set a new standard that is going to be difficult for any team to match. I have never seen players help each other out like these guys do.

"When I played football, I wanted to be the one that scored the most points and had the most yards gained. I wanted to be the one with my picture in the paper making some fantastic run. It was all about me. I seldom thought about my teammates -- except how they could help me look better. I was selfish and I was bent on seeking personal glory, but not these boys. When someone scores, it is a team score. When someone makes a good play, it's because the whole team did their jobs. These are the most humble players I've ever known. I thank you guys for teaching me a valuable lesson that I wish I would have learned a long time ago. We have all benefited from watching you this season. I congratulate you!

"Now, having said that, I have been asked by the State High School Athletic Association to present an award to our Jordan football team. As you know, they previously received a trophy for winning the conference championship, which is on display in the high school trophy case. But at the completion of the season, the association, which is composed of twenty-four members or judges, carefully reviewed each team's performance over the course of the season based on attitude and conduct. I was told that when the judges watched the video tape of our Jordan players helping their opponents off the field when they had been injured, when they saw our players shake the hand of each official after the games and thank them for a good job, and when they saw our guys endure insults and ridicule without responding, they unanimously voted to give the Good Sportsmanship Award to our Jordan football team. And just for the record book, this is the first time in State history that the vote has been unanimous. So congratulations to our team!"

The crowd rose and gave a big round of applause for the team. Ben was totally surprised by this announcement. He didn't even know that such an award existed. Receiving that award was certainly a great climax to their season.

Chapter 39

Mrs. Brown rose and introduced the last speaker for the evening. "Tonight we are also honored to have Mr. Phelps, our School Board President, speak to us. He has been a board member for twelve years and has faithfully worked to keep our school district in good standing. He is a familiar face to many of us. Please welcome Mr. Phelps." Ben noticed the rather sober look on Mr. Phelps's face as he walked to the front. He hoped this wasn't a sign of bad things to come.

"In conjunction with the other speakers I too want to congratulate this team and Coach Harper on a phenomenal season! After the last few seasons, who would ever have thought that such a complete turnaround was even possible? I commend all of you for your courage and hard work. I am truly amazed at what you've accomplished.

"I find it amusing that sometimes we learn the most important things from people we think are the least likely to teach us anything. I had never met Coach Harper until a few weeks ago. I didn't anticipate that I would really learn anything from him, but I was wrong. One thing he talked about, as we've heard tonight, is the issue of integrity. I had never really thought about being a man of integrity until I heard Coach Harper. I think I always believed that I was such a man, but I had never really focused on it.

"What is integrity? I believe it means to be honest, to be trustworthy, and to stand firm for what is right. You can probably add some other ideas of your own, but these are the concepts that come to my mind when I think about being a man of integrity. As your elected School Board member and president, I'm convicted that if I'm going to be a man of integrity, I need to be up front with all of you."

Ben suddenly felt his stomach churning. This did not have the appearance of a good ending.

"Normally, I would not speak at an event like this. The previous speakers have done a great job in honoring this team. But there is a matter that has come up before the School Board. Since we have nearly everyone from the school here tonight, I felt it would be best to inform everyone at once.

"Several weeks ago it was brought to the attention of the School Board that Coach Harper was praying on the football field with his team before each game. As you know, the State has specific rules that we must follow or we jeopardize losing our State aid. We've had to modify our procedures on some things over the years to comply with various rules, but it has never been a problem. Obviously, if we lose our State aid, then we are in dire straits. We've been struggling the way it is to meet our budget each year. Every teacher is made aware at the time of hire that they are not allowed to talk about God or to pray with their students on school property. That is one of the State's rules and they are very strict about it. We discussed this issue with Coach Harper at one of our School Board meetings. He contends, and he is correct, that the football field is not school property. When the school was originally built, the School Board purchased property form the Dawson family. However, there were insufficient funds at the time to purchase enough land for a football field. So, to overcome the problem, the Dawson family graciously allowed us to rent the property for a minimal amount. And we have continued to do that to the present time. Therefore, technically the property does not belong to the school, and technically Mr. Harper has not been praying on school property.

"I have seen firsthand what a terrific job Mr. Harper has done with his students and players. I have personally attended and participated in his science class, I have observed the conduct of his players on the field, and I have checked the grades of most of his students. It is all positive. It is remarkable that he has been able to accomplish all of these things in such a short time. But, we presented our situation to the State for their ruling, just to make sure we weren't in violation. Last week we received their written response. Even though we don't own the football field property, they still view it as being in our possession because of the lease agreement. Therefore, their ruling is, unless Mr. Harper agrees to stop praying on the football field, he must be terminated from his coaching position at Jordan High."

The room suddenly turned into chaos as everyone objected to the ruling Mr. Phelps just explained. It was obvious that no one wanted Ben terminated. Mr. Phelps raised his hand to quiet the crowd. When order was finally restored, he said, "I'm afraid our hands are tied. There is no way we can operate without State aid, and that is the outcome if Mr. Harper is allowed to continue as he has." Then Mr. Phelps turned to Ben. "Mr. Harper, this all seems so trivial. If you are willing to stop praying with your players, then we no longer have a problem and we can move forward."

In the midst of this whole chaotic situation Ben had been thinking how sad it was that such a joyful celebration had suddenly become such a controversial meeting. He had worked hard to cultivate a good relationship with these players and with his students, and he knew it was only because of God's direction in his life. He strongly believed that this prayer time with the boys had helped them all to focus on what really mattered, bringing honor to God. Prayer had become a critical part of who they were. Ben had heard his name, but had missed the question. "I'm sorry Mr. Phelps, could you repeat the question?"

"Mr. Harper, are you willing to stop praying with your players so that we can resolve this issue? The State Board of Education wants an answer so they can justify that the issue has been eliminated." The crowd became extremely quiet as Ben now stood up. You could have heard a pin drop as everyone waited to hear Ben's response.

"Mr. Phelps, I believe that in some unknown way God works in the life of every person to accomplish what He wants accomplished. God has a master plan and we are all part of that plan, whether we think we are or not. When I was in college I accepted Christ as my Savior. That meant I became a player on

God's team. God became my coach. A coach has certain responsibilities. He is supposed to provide direction and training. He is supposed to be concerned about his players and help them in their weaknesses. He is to be there for his team and encourage them. Players have the privilege of receiving all these benefits. Players also have the privilege of talking to their coach. They can ask questions, discuss ideas, express concerns, and seek help. A coach delights when his players talk to him. If one of my players were to stop talking to me, I would know that something was wrong and I would be very disappointed.

"So, my point is this. If God is the leader, the coach of this team, doesn't it make sense to talk to Him? To get directions from Him? To seek help from Him? To me that is the least I can do. I want to be a part of the greatest team on earth, God's team. I can't do that unless I talk to Him, unless I pray to Him. When I pray with these boys on the football field, I don't pray that God will allow them to win the game. I honestly doubt that whether they win or lose really matters to God. I pray that God will help these boys to play in a way that will honor Him, to play by the 10 rules we spoke of earlier. If we can accomplish that, then I believe we will bring honor to God, and that God will bless us. As a player on God's team, I cannot stop talking or praying to Him. He is my coach. I don't want to disappoint Him.

"When I was called to the School Board meeting a few weeks ago, I made a commitment to all of the Board members. The commitment was that I be allowed to continue praying with the boys on the field; and that if by the end of the season you did not see a big improvement in the boys' conduct, attitude, and grades, then I would resign not only as football coach but as a teacher at Jordan High. My belief was that if I couldn't help these boys in these areas and help them to honor God through prayer, then I was not successful as a football coach or as a teacher. But as everyone has testified tonight, all of these things have happened. Therefore, I believe that I have fulfilled my commitment. So, to answer your question, if I am allowed to continue coaching, I will not stop praying with my team."

Ben sat down and the silence prevailed. It almost seemed that the crowd was paralyzed. Ben had made a bold stand for what he believed. That was not a common thing for most of these people. Ben then heard gentle clapping from the end of the row. His players were starting to clap in support of their coach. Their clapping was getting louder. Then they stood and clapped even stronger. Soon the entire audience was standing and clapping. Ben was humbled to the point of tears as he witnessed the support of so many people.

Finally Mr. Phelps raised his hand and motioned for the people to sit. "Mr. Harper, I don't think anyone disputes the fact that you have changed these boys in remarkable ways. But losing our state funding if you are allowed to continue is something we just cannot forfeit. Therefore, if you are firm in your position, it seems as though we have no choice but to terminate Mr. Harper as an employee of Jordan High School."

With that statement the crowd started booing and yelling, "You can't do that." We want Mr. Harper to stay." "That's not fair."

From seemingly nowhere Ruth stood near the back of the room. Ben didn't even know she was present. The crowd slowly noticed her and soon became silent. "Mr. Phelps, I served on the school board for many years when I was younger, and I know how hard it is to balance regulations with the reality of what makes sense. I remember, however, that there is a provision in the State Board of Education regulations that allows any school district to override almost any State requirement, without penalty, if it is approved by a unanimous vote of all School Board members. I've never heard of it being used before, but it might be worth a vote, since I sense most people are in favor of keeping Mr. Harper on staff."

"Ruth, you are correct. I remember reading that a couple months ago, but brushed it off. We have a problem though, only ten of our twelve members are here tonight. One is out of town and one is home sick."

Ruth suggested, "Mr. Phelps, you could try and call them. They might be willing to vote over the phone if you explained the situation to them."

"That's a good idea. If I could have all the Board Members meet with me in this conference room, we will try to contact the other two members and discuss this issue."

After about twenty minutes the Board Members returned to the main auditorium. Mr. Phelps approached the microphone to address the crowd. As he did, Ben realized he had a huge knot in his stomach again. He was fearful that his job as a teacher and as a coach was probably finished. Implementing a procedure that had never been used before on a topic that was so controversial at an impromptu meeting with two board members absent didn't seem likely to have a favorable outcome.

Mr. Phelps began, "We were able to contact our two absent Board Members and I am pleased to announce that the vote was unanimous to allow Coach Harper to pray with his team. In fact we voted to allow all of our coaches to pray with their team members as long as no team member is forced to pray with the group."

The audience rose in applause at the announcement. Ben couldn't believe what just happened. God had brought another victory to Jordan – one that could potentially change the lives of many young people. Ben remembered the Bible verse in Luke, "Nothing is impossible with God."[23] Ben offered a quick prayer of thanks and then shook the hand of all his players, including Bobby. The rest of the evening was a blur in Ben's mind. But his eyes had been opened that night as he witnessed a miracle happen in the town of Jordan.

---

[23] Lk. 1:37 – "For with God nothing will be impossible." (NKJV)

Chapter 40

The next two weeks of school went by quickly as everyone prepared for Christmas break. Ben had several tests to give, so he was quite busy. He was looking forward to the upcoming three week vacation from school. He needed some time off. These first few months of his new job had been quite a ride, to say the least.

Ben decided to go back to Cleveland over break, to re-connect with family and friends. It was time now. God had begun the healing process, and he felt much more prepared to talk with people than when he left. God had given him a new mission for his life, and that had really helped.

The last day of school ended on Thursday, but Ben had some cleanup to do in his room at school on Friday before leaving on break. He went to school about 9:00 in the morning and was making good progress, when he heard his door open. "Good morning, Coach," Buck quietly called out as he opened the door and saw Ben working diligently. "Am I disturbing you?"

"No, Buck, you are not disturbing me. I always like to talk to my students. Do you have big plans for Christmas break?"

"Nothing too big, I guess. I'm planning to spend some extra time with my mom. Our relationship has really improved since school started, since I changed my attitude and decided being a jerk wasn't how God wanted me to live my life!"

"That's great, Buck. I'm glad things are going well. I've really appreciated getting to know you these past few months."

"Yeah, Coach. I really want to thank you for helping me get my life on a better track. Thank you too, for being our football coach this season. I know you didn't want to do it at first, but you really helped us all see how important team work is. Thank you."

"You are welcome, Buck, but I think you guys helped me more than I helped you."

"Coach, can I show you something?"

"Sure Buck, what do you have?"

"After I donated bone marrow for Bobby, I got a little interested in DNA and how that is passed along from parents to children. I requested a copy of my DNA test results from the hospital, since I thought it might be interesting to see how I rated! Well, I discovered that it is far more complicated that I can understand."

"I hope you didn't come here thinking I could interpret your DNA test results for you! I like science, but I'm certainly not a medical professional."

"No, Coach, I didn't expect an interpretation, but I think they gave me more information than they were supposed to give me. I noticed at the bottom of the report it has boxes for 'parental match', 'relative match', 'sibling match', 'half sibling match'. The box marked 'sibling match' is checked. Does that mean I'm Bobby's brother?"

After studying the paper, Ben said, "I think you're right, Buck. Remember the nurse said you were almost a perfect match?"

"Does that mean my mom is also Bobby's mom or am I adopted too? I'm almost ten years older than Bobby. Doesn't it seem unlikely that parents would have two kids that far apart and give both of them up for adoption?"

"Well, stranger things have happened! When I first heard that you were a match for Bobby, I wondered then if you might be brothers, but I didn't think it was my place to suggest the possibility."

"Coach, what do I do with this now?"

"I think the real question is 'What do you want to do with it?'"

"I want to run over there right now and tell Bobby that we are brothers. I want to be a part of his life. It's like we've missed ten years of being together. I want to find out if I'm adopted also. Has my mom been hiding this from me all these years?"

"Maybe you should just take it slow and start spending more time with Bobby. Talk to his mom and dad, and talk to your mom. These things can be sensitive issues, but I'm confident God will show you when the time is right. Remember, nothing is too difficult for God.[24]"

"You are right, Coach. Thanks for the advice. I think I have some Christmas shopping to do. Have a nice Christmas!"

"You too, Buck. May it be your best one ever!"

---

[24] Jer 32:27 – "Behold, I am the Lord, the God of all flesh. Is anything too hard for Me?" (NIV)

Chapter 41

As Ben left town on Saturday morning he stopped at Ruth's house to drop off the rent check for January, since he would be out of town when the first of the month came around. As always, Ruth had a glowing smile on her face as she opened the door to greet Ben. "Please come in, Ben. I'm making some chocolate chip cookies. You can take some with you on your trip." Ben politely resisted, but Ruth never took no for an answer. Of course as he waited for Ruth to put some in a bag, he had to sample a couple warm ones just out of the oven. Ruth did make the best cookies!

"Ruth, I want to thank you for your support at the meeting the other night. You saved my life!"

"It wasn't me, Ben. I just received a nudge from the Holy Spirit and knew I had to speak up. God had it under control all along! I'm proud of you, Ben. You stood firm for what is right, and God honored you. You've made a huge impact on the lives of many people here in Jordan. Keep up the good work!"

"Thank you, Ruth. You are a good encourager."

"Rule #2, right?" They both laughed. Ben hugged her and wished her a Merry Christmas. Ben drove away with his bag of cookies, thankful that God had made Ruth his landlord and his good friend.

As Ben was leaving town, the City sign caught his eye. "Thank you for visiting Jordan. Please come back." He pulled over for a minute and recalled when he first entered Jordan several months ago and saw this sign from the other direction, "Welcome to Jordan." That day was still vivid in his mind. He remembered the thought of the Israelites crossing the Jordan into a promised land. Because the river closed behind them, there was no turning back. The new land was filled with many battles, but God's hand of provision was more apparent with each passing victory. Ben remembered the battles he'd been through: Mr. Reed, the school Principal; opening week with the students; Mr. Baxter, the sports editor for the newspaper; and Mr. Phelps, the School Board President. In all cases God had brought victory. Peoples' hearts had been changed. Crossing Jordan hadn't been easy, but the results were good. Ben's own heart had been changed in the process also. He was now able to move on from losing Amy, though emotions still flooded his soul at times. God had brought him to this place for a reason – for healing, both for himself and for many others. He sensed that God was using him to touch the lives of other people, and that felt good.

In his nostalgia he almost missed it. Underneath the City sign someone had attached a smaller sign neatly painted with the words "Remember our rules -- ieb-sw-lepte."

APPENDIX

BIBLE VERSES FOR 10 RULES

Our Purpose: To bring glory to God in all things.

- Rom. 11:36 – For everything comes from God alone, everything lives by His power, and everything is for His glory. To Him be glory evermore (LB).
- Rev. 4:11 – You are worthy, our Lord and God, to receive glory and honor and power, for you created all things, and by your will they were created and have their being (NIV).

Our Standard: I will live by a higher standard than the world lives by.

- Rom. 12:2a – Do not conform to the pattern of this world, but be transformed by the renewing of your mind (NIV).
- I Pet. 1:14 – As obedient children, do not conform to the evil desires you had when you lived in ignorance (NIV).
- Eph. 4:17 – Live no longer as the ungodly do, for they are hopelessly confused (NLT).

Our Rules:

1. I will be a man of integrity.
   - I Chron. 29:17a – I know, my God, that you test the heart and are pleased with integrity (NIV).
2. I will encourage others.
   - Heb. 3:13 – But encourage one another daily, as long as it is called "Today", so that none of you may be hardened by sin's deceitfulness. (NIV).
   - I Thes. 5:11 – Therefore encourage one another and build each other up, just as in fact you are doing (NIV).
3. I will bear others burdens.

- Gal. 6:2 – Bear one another's burdens, and so fulfill the law of Christ (NKJV).
- Phil. 2:3-4 – Do nothing out of selfish ambition or vain conceit. Rather in humility value others above yourselves, not looking to your own interests but each of you to the interests of others (NIV).

4. I will not speak unwholesome words.
   - Eph. 4:29 – Do not let any unwholesome talk come out of your mouths, but only what is helpful for building others up according to their needs, that it may benefit those who listen (NIV).
   - Phil 2:14 – Do everything without complaining or arguing (NIV).
   - Col. 3:8 – But now you must rid yourselves of all such things as these: anger, rage, malice, slander, and filthy language from your lips (NIV).
   - Ex. 20:7 – You shall not misuse the name of the Lord your God, for the Lord will not hold anyone guiltless who misuses His name (NIV).

5. I will work hard.
   - Col. 3:23-24 – Whatever you do, work at it with all your heart, as working for the Lord, not for human masters, since you know that you will receive an inheritance from the Lord as a reward. It is the Lord Christ you are serving (NIV).
   - Eph. 6:6-7 – Work hard, but not just to please your masters when they are watching. As slaves of Christ, do the will of God with all your heart. Work with enthusiasm, as though you were working for the Lord rather than for people (NLT).

- Gen. 2:15 – The Lord God took the man and put him in the Garden of Eden to work it and take care of it (NIV).

6. **I will love my enemies.**

- Lk. 6:27-28 – But to you who are listening I say: Love your enemies, do good to those who hate you, bless those who curse you, pray for those who mistreat you (NIV).
- Eph. 4:32 – Be kind and compassionate to one another, forgiving each other, just as in Christ God forgave you (NIV).
- Col. 3:13 – Bear with each other and forgive one another if any of you has a grievance against someone. Forgive as the Lord forgave you (NIV).

7. **I will endure insults.**

- I Pet. 2:22-23 – He never sinned, never told a lie, never answered back when insulted; when he suffered he did not threaten to get even; he left his case in the hands of God who always judges fairly (LB).
- Phil. 1:28a – Don't be intimidated by your enemies (NLT).

8. **I will not pollute my body.**

- I Cor. 6:19-20 – Haven't you yet learned that your body is the home of the Holy Spirit God gave you, and that he lives within you? Your own body does not belong to you. For God has bought you with a great price. So use every part of your body to give glory back to God because he owns it (LB).
- Rom. 6:12-13 – Therefore do not let sin reign in your mortal body so that you obey its evil desires. Do not offer any part of yourself to sin as

instruments of wickedness, but rather offer yourselves to God as those who have been brought from death to life; and offer every part of yourself to him as an instrument of righteousness (NIV).

9. I will be a team player.

- Rom. 12:3-5 -- For by the grace given me I say to every one of you: Do not think of yourself more highly than you ought, but rather think of yourself with sober judgment, in accordance with the faith God has distributed to each of you. For just as each of us has one body with many members, and these members do not all have the same function, so in Christ we, though many, form one body, and each member belongs to all the others (NIV).

- Phil. 2:3-4 – Don't be selfish; don't live to make a good impression on others. Be humble, thinking of others as better than yourself. Don't think only about your own affairs, but be interested in others, too, and what they are doing (NLT).

10. I will enjoy life.

- Eccl. 3:12-13 -- So I conclude that, first, there is nothing better for a man than to be happy and to enjoy himself as long as he can; and second, that he should eat and drink and enjoy the fruits of his labors, for these are gifts from God (LB).

- Phil. 4:4 – Always be full of joy in the Lord. I say it again - rejoice! (NLT).

Made in the USA
Monee, IL
21 September 2021